In Search
of a Story

In Search
of a Story

Short stories

by

Daphne de Jong

marmac
media

Marmac Media
29 Randwick Crescent
Lower Hutt, Wellington. 5010
www.marmacmedia.com

In Search of a Story / Daphne de Jong – 1st ed.
ISBN 978-0-1-99-118546-4 paperback
ISBN 978-0-1-99-118547-1 epub

CONTENTS

AN HONOURABLE MAN

"Jack's dead." Colin glanced over his newspaper.

On the other side of the table Marie looked up briefly, then finished spreading Marmite onto her toast.

"You remember Jack."

"Of course I remember him." Marie cut the toast precisely in half.

"The Dutchie that used to be at the factory with me."

"I told you I remember." His name wasn't really Jack. It was something long and Dutch. But he'd been Jack since he came to New Zealand and was sent to work alongside Colin at the local dairy factory.

"There's no family mentioned."

"None?" Surprised, Marie put down the knife. "You sure it's him?"

Colin chuckled. "With that tongue-tangling name and 'Jack' in brackets? Got to be him."

Marie imagined a service with no one there, a lone coffin. "We should go."

"Go…?"

"To the funeral."

Colin was reading again, down the list of deaths. These days it was the first page he looked at.

Marie got up to put on the jug and take down the coffee from the cupboard. "I'd like to know what happened to him."

The church was a Catholic one, quite large and more than half full. The coffin was dark, polished wood with silver handles, one white lily lying on the closed lid. No other flowers. The death notice had suggested donations to the Cancer Society.

Colin gazed about and nudged Marie. "There's Dick. Dick Blake, the foreman. Used to give old Jack a hard time for his accent."

"I know." Jack hadn't been old then, but a young man with a fresh, innocent face, and far away from home. She remembered a staff party with wives and partners, the foreman telling a story about Jack getting some English word wrong and shocking the boss's secretary, and everyone had laughed. Jack had laughed too in a slightly bewildered way, and his fair complexion reddened. "He's blushing!" Dick roared with glee, and clapped the younger man on the back, then poured more beer into Jack's glass, promising, "We'll make a Kiwi of you yet."

"Is that what you want?" Marie asked Jack a little later, standing next to him at the supper table. "To be a Kiwi?"

"Yes," Jack said earnestly. "I would like to be a natural-ised citizen of New Zealand. That is my ambition. And to speak good English, like Dick and your husband...Colin?"

"Yes, Colin Sykes. And I'm Marie."

"Jack is my name," he told her, and offered his hand. When she put hers in it, he gripped it firmly.

Marie smiled. "But is that your real name?"

He shook his head, letting go of her hand. "Jack is my New Zealand name. I am going to be a New Zealander. A Kiwi. Please, I can fetch for you a cup of tea?"

But she'd already sent Colin off to get her one.

On the way home after the party Marie said, "You should invite Jack around sometime."

Colin teased, "Fancy him, do you?"

"Don't be silly." Not that Jack wasn't good-looking, with his innocent blue eyes and sandy curls. He had to be over twenty-one, but seemed younger.

Marie and Colin had been married only a couple of years and she had just stopped suffering from morning sickness with her first pregnancy. "We should be nice to him. He must be lonely."

"Yeah, all right. I'll ask him if he wants to come for tea one night, if you like."

Jack came to tea, sat stiffly at the table and politely answered questions about his family and the Netherlands and what he thought of New Zealand. Afterwards he insisted on helping Marie with the dishes, although he didn't seem particularly good at it. She asked if he did the dishes back home and he looked guilty and confessed, "No, my sisters did them." He'd come from a farming background, and had helped his father on the farm until he'd emigrated. He had three sisters, and an older brother who would inherit the farm.

The next time he visited he brought photographs: his brother, his sisters, his mother and father, and the old thatched farmhouse. Colin shuffled through them quickly with a pretence of interest, but Marie was fascinated by the solid brick house with a thatched roof, and by Jack's description of the sleeping arrangements. His sisters had slept in cupboard beds in the living room where the big fireplace was, while Jack and his brother shared an attic under the thatch.

The service began and the priest announced that they were here to give thanks for Jack's life. He said the congregation's thoughts were with Jack's remaining family in the Netherlands, who had not been able to make the trip to his funeral. And that Jack had gone to join his brother who had died some years ago in their homeland.

Marie imagined a midnight call to Jack from the other side of the world, a tinny voice announcing that his brother was dead. Had there been anyone to comfort him? Were his sisters alive? Had they kept in touch with him? He'd said on their first meeting that he was the youngest. "Very much younger. The...the *later overweging,*" he told her, looking frustrated. She'd tried not to giggle, but Jack had laughed too, really laughed.

"I'm sorry," Marie said.

"No, not sorry."

"You were an afterthought?" she guessed. "A surprise."

"I think. After...thought. Ah! That is funny, yes?"

They were both giggling when Colin came back with her tea.

The priest said, "And our sympathy also goes out to Thelma and Don Adler and their family, who have lost their very good friend and neighbour, and to all his other friends gathered here today."

When they got to the eulogy given by the long-time neighbour, Marie learned that after moving away, Jack had worked as a salesman in a hardware shop, then as a head storeman until he was made redundant. Unemployed, he'd spent his time doing volunteer work with young people, and continued that in later years. "Jack never had a family of his own," Don Adler said. "He never married. But he loved kids."

In the front pew with Mr and Mrs Adler a young woman with a baby in her arms sobbed, and the man sitting beside her put an arm about her shoulders, murmuring into her ear.

Yes. When he'd noticed Marie was pregnant, Jack had said nothing, but as she went to lift a basket of washing out of the way so she could set the table he'd rushed to take it from her, and the next time he came to tea he brought a huge pink teddy bear wrapped in cellophane.

"But," he said anxiously, "the boys at work told me pink is for a girl. Is wrong?"

Touched, Marie assured him that the baby wouldn't care. Then she grimaced and put a hand to her stomach and he gave her a worried look. "You have pain?"

"The baby's kicking," she told him, and laughed. "I think I've got a little All Black in there."

He laughed too, and looked at her stomach. "One day I would like to have a little All Black. A real Kiwi baby."

"I'm sure you will," she told him. "A whole team maybe—if you can persuade your wife."

"I think she might not like that. In the Netherlands we have big families, but my wife will be a Kiwi."

"Have you met someone?" Marie asked him.

"Not yet. I have not enough money now. Later."

"Well, I hope you find a really nice Kiwi girl."

Marie and Colin's two children didn't remember Jack. He'd left when Danny was nearly three and Melissa was a few months old. But he had been almost as thrilled as Marie and Colin when Danny was born. He'd been one of her first visitors, bringing a blue teddy bear and bearing an enormous bunch of flowers. She'd laughed at him and protested, "I told you the pink teddy was fine—you shouldn't have spent all that money on us!"

"For a future All Black," he said, "is not too much. And for his mother. Colin is so much pleased with you. You look very...wonderful."

"Thank you." She was wearing a dress she'd been saving and had put on makeup and brushed her hair. "At least I'm not fat any more."

"You were not fat," Jack said almost sternly. "You were pregnant and that is beautiful." Then he blushed and Marie laughed again. "That's sweet of you, Jack."

He'd been enchanted by the baby, and when Marie stopped breastfeeding he'd diffidently offered to babysit, a bit nervous about the responsibility but willing. And they'd left him with a list of instructions and a telephone number and gone off to visit friends. After that Jack quite often looked after Danny, and later his sister too. When they were awake he played with them, and he often brought them little presents and treats. But they'd forgotten all that now. Maybe he'd forgotten too, after he moved away.

Another man came to the lectern. In a heavy Dutch accent he told how he had met Jack on the journey to New Zealand, and though they lived in different parts of the country they had never lost touch. Jack, as he called himself, was a good man, an honourable man, a wonderful friend.

Marie felt a small stab of jealousy. She and Colin had not heard from Jack after he resigned from the factory and left their town for a bigger, more prosperous one. He hadn't even acknowledged her Christmas cards. She had assumed he was making new friends, perhaps a girlfriend, in time, probably a wife and children. Everything he'd wanted.

The scent of incense filled the church, and the coffin was carried out. Marie and Colin got up and shuffled after it with the other mourners, pausing to speak to the Adlers, who seemed the nearest thing to family that Jack had in his adopted country. The young mother was their daughter Jane, still moist-eyed and being patted on her shoulder by her husband, who had taken the baby into his other arm.

"We were at Jack's citizenship ceremony," Marie told them. Before he moved away they had been invited to watch him take the oath and proudly receive the certificate that made him a bona fide Kiwi.

Mrs Adler looked very interested. "You must come along to the house. Jack would have been so pleased that you're here."

Colin went over to say hello to Dick Blake, his and Jack's ex-foreman. When he came back to Marie he said, "You don't want to go to the cemetery, do you?"

"Maybe we should. We've been invited to the Adlers'. I've got the address."

They debated as the hearse moved off. Colin sighed, "Okay then. I hope they give us a decent feed."

"Colin!"

"Well, I'm hungry."

There was a cool breeze at the cemetery. The group of mourners had shrunk. Marie's best high heels sank into the damp earth, and the priest's garments stirred about his stocky figure as he read prayers from a black book. Jane wept again, and Mrs Adler was wiping her eyes too.

Afterwards they found the house and joined perhaps near a hundred people inside or standing on a large well-trimmed lawn where some tables and chairs had been placed. Colin hoed into sandwiches and savouries. Marie accepted a coffee from Jane, who had stopped crying. The baby was asleep, she said. "I'm glad Uncle Jack lived long enough to see him. He just loved children. Mum said you knew him when he first came to New Zealand."

"Yes," Marie agreed. "He used to look after our children too, when they were little. I'm surprised he never married."

"Yes, it's a shame. Mum said—Well..." The younger woman looked away, and shrugged.

Marie took the plunge. "He told me he wanted to marry a nice Kiwi girl and have a family. Did he ever have a girlfriend?" Not when she knew him. He would have told her. Colin had even teased him about it, but Jack said he needed to improve his "NewZealandish", find a better-paid job and get his citizenship first.

"Well," Jane said, "apparently, he went out with girls when he was young. One of them was broken-hearted—she'd thought he'd pop the question. And when he didn't...I gather she was a bit of a drama queen." Again Jane shrugged. "Mum thinks he felt so guilty he gave up."

"So she was the wrong girl. That's no reason..."

Jane gave a sad little laugh, then cut it off and shook her head. "I wasn't supposed to tell, but he's gone now, so it doesn't matter, I guess. And maybe you knew her."

"Knew...who?"

"The love of his life. He told Mum he'd met someone and he'd vowed to find a Kiwi bride like her, only—" Jane momentarily lifted her shoulders.

"What? She *turned* him *down*? How could anyone do that to a man like Jack? Does she still live here?" Marie looked around as if to find the woman. Colin was talking to Dick Blake and the old Dutch man with the hearty, rolling accent.

"Oh no," Jane assured her. "I don't think she's here. It was when he worked in the dairy factory with your husband. I thought you might know?"

"But—" The cup Marie held stopped halfway to her mouth. Jack would have told her and Colin if he'd had a girlfriend. She knew he would.

"What?" Jane asked. "You didn't know?"

Marie shook her head. "No."

The Dutch man wandered off, and Colin and Dick Blake turned to join Marie. "Hello." Colin nodded to the Adler daughter.

"Jack was in love with a married woman," Marie realised.

Colin gave her an odd look.

Dick Blake laughed. "The boss's secretary. Good-looking girl, she was." He looked as though he was inwardly smacking his lips. "Trouble, though. Felt quite sorry for young Jack," he admitted to Colin, "that time you sorted him out."

"What time?" Marie stared at Colin.

He shrugged uncomfortably. "It's years ago. I've forgotten. Dick, how about a beer? I think there's some—"

But even beer wasn't going to deflect Dick. "Course you remember! You and Jack mixing it in the caf, with Jack swearing in Dutch and yelling about some men not appreciating what they had, and the office girl screaming blue murder and then denying everything when the boss asked what Jack had been up to with her. Ask me, the little bitch prob'ly led him on for a bit of fun. Never seen Jack so worked up." Dick grinned and winked at Marie. "But he soon calmed down when old Col here gave him a bloody nose."

Marie felt a jolt in her midriff. "You never said!" she accused Colin. "When was this?"

"You wouldn't have wanted to know," he told her, his face flushing. "It was after Melissa was born and you weren't interested in anything." His voice was almost accusing.

She'd been exhausted all the time with the new baby and a toddler, hardly known what day it was. And Colin had been working a lot of overtime. He'd taken to having a drink or two with his mates a couple of days a week, before coming home to help. It had not been a good time in their marriage.

"Was she like that?" Marie asked him. "The woman. A...a tease? Would she have led him on?" What a waste if Jack had spent his whole life looking back to someone like that.

"No," Colin said, staring at Dick. "She was...well, a nice girl. A sympathetic sort of woman. You couldn't blame any man for...for liking her."

"Whoever she was," Jane said, "Jack probably never said anything to her about how he felt."

Colin put his hands in his pockets and rocked slightly. "If he had," he said, "her husband would have punched his face in."

"Or she might have run away with him," Jane suggested.

Colin looked almost startled. Then he said, "I suppose she might have." He looked at his wife. "Do you think she would have, Marie?"

"How would I know?" Marie stared blankly at him, and then suddenly it was like being back in the cemetery, with the cold breeze blowing as Jack's coffin was lowered into the waiting earth.

"I don't know," she said thinly, tears rising in her throat. "I really don't know. Like Jane said, he never would have asked. He was...an honourable man."

BOUGAINVILLEA

Ellen put the last dish into the drainer and pulled the plug on a sink-full of greasy, coffee-coloured water. Outside a white butterfly hovered over the bougainvillea on the fence, drifted in a lazy loop and then swooped on the neighbour's cabbages.

All the kids were at school, and Ellen should be using her time productively. Instead she stood looking out the window and thought about butterflies, spending their lives in apparently aimless flight, but in fact profligately laying their eggs anywhere they landed—dozens, hundreds of eggs. Ensuring the survival of their species.

This morning's *Herald* said the New Zealand birth rate wasn't high enough now to replace the population. Ellen and Toby had replaced themselves twice over. Some people thought four was a big family.

Daylight saving had nearly ended but the bougainvillea still bloomed, scrambling over the sagging boards of a wooden fence that was the same tired, dreary grey as the looming sky.

When she was trimming the plant last autumn, Ellen had got a thorn in her foot. Even though she immediately pulled the barb out, the tiny wound throbbed all night and stopped her from sleeping. Since then, she'd not felt quite the same about the exotic, brash explosion of summer colour. Roses gave mere pinpricks compared with the savage spearing of a bougainvillea.

It had been one of the minor mistakes of her life: planting it along the newly erected back fence when she and Toby moved into the subdivision's two-bedroom box that was all they could afford. Toby dug up the hard clay the developers had left bare, and seeded a lawn, while Ellen ambitiously bought bulbs and perennials and spent weekends up to her elbows in dirt and GrowFast.

Sixteen years and four children had leached her enthusiasm from her, just as the clay had leached away the compost and fertiliser she'd once lavished upon it. The bougainvillea, planted in the wrong place, had been a danger to the children when they were small.

"Yes, pretty, but don't touch—it's prickly. There! See? I told you not to!"

It had sprawled all along the fence, blooming more profusely each year, its rampant beauty bringing Ellen a rush of pleasure when she stood at the sink scraping new potatoes or scrubbing a burnt pot.

She'd never let Toby chop it out. Instead he'd built a chicken-wire barrier that eventually fell down. By then the children were older and it wasn't needed any more.

This place was supposed to be their starter house. They'd talked of buying something bigger when their first baby was born, but prices kept rising and their savings never caught up.

Lily would be fifteen next birthday, and when not sulking in her room was hanging out with friends, wearing a bottom-hugging micro-skirt or skinny hipsters, and calling herself 'Delilah'. Ellen was trapped between Lily's struggle for independence and Toby's increasing irritation and alarm that his only daughter was growing up.

When Lily got her navel pierced and slipped a silver ring into it, there was a row. Afterwards, alone with Toby in their bed, Ellen said, "Look on the bright side. It's not in her lip or her eyebrow."

Toby said it was Ellen's fault—she'd taken Lily to get her ears pierced for her thirteenth birthday and that's where it started. Then he hunched the blankets over his shoulders and turned his back to go to sleep.

Toby wasn't good at looking on the bright side.

Ellen hoped her daughter would go to university. Lily was doing well at school. At her age Ellen had slacked; couldn't wait to get out of school and get a job, couldn't wait to get married when she met Toby, couldn't wait for their first home—and their first mortgage.

They'd had to get a second mortgage when they needed to build another room for the boys, and then when their old car clapped out. The pill never agreed with Ellen, so Toby persuaded her to have her tubes tied. She hadn't expected to mourn for children she didn't want and would never know, but for months—years—she'd had pangs of a strange, tearing grief whenever she saw a newborn.

She couldn't shake the feeling there was something faintly perverse in thwarting nature.

Stupid, of course. People pull weeds from the garden, cut down trees for timber and paper, castrate animals, and remove calves from their mothers so the milk goes to human babies—and to adults.

Why should grown-up human beings need baby food? Surely it was unnatural? Yet what would they do without it?

Running on automatic, Ellen crossed the small kitchen to stare into the fridge. A packet of supermarket mince sat in a plastic tray, oozing a watery pink puddle. Curried mince on rice would do for tea—mild because the boys didn't like it too hot.

The room had darkened; raindrops spattered the window. She took sheets from the hot water cupboard in the narrow hall and started stripping the queen-size bed in the so-called master bedroom, hardly swinging-cat size. You had to squeeze between the bed and the dressing table to get to the wardrobe.

Ellen used to gaze longingly through magazine pictures of bedrooms that had acres of floor dressed with ankle-deep white rugs, and windows framed by elegantly pleated drapes. The king-size beds were covered in satin and accessorised with plump, tasselled cushions—and a gorgeous robe apparently carelessly tossed on the corner of the bed, miraculously landing in artistic folds.

Fantasy. Even thinking of that kind of house when you had a family only led to frustration and dissatisfaction.

It was enough to have happy, healthy children, a solid marriage to a good man who loved her, and a roof over their heads. Years ago she'd bought a satin-look bedspread, dull gold with a lovely sheen. She'd folded it every night, but one day carelessly put a baby boy down on the bed for a minute, wrapped in a towel that was no protection when he peed, copiously. A year later the then three-year-old, after whining about a tummy ache, had vomited over the folded spread. Despairing of ever removing the stain, she'd cut it out and used the remaining fabric to make a fairy princess dress for Lily when she was seven. In the lounge was a photo of Lily wearing it, with a gold plastic crown on her curls and holding a wand with a gold star covered in glitter.

Now all Lily's clothes had labels on them. She'd just *die* if she had to wear something home-sewn.

Ellen had thought it might be good for Lily to learn what clothes cost, especially clothes with trendy labels. She'd persuaded Toby they should give Lily an allowance, then had to cope with Toby's disapproval of what Lily spent it on. Ellen knew that sometimes when Lily left the house in a baggy T-shirt and jeans, underneath there'd be a skimpy top and bottom-hugging micro-skirt, the outer layer to be removed as soon as she was out of sight of home.

Lily had no puppy fat despite the fullness of her firm young breasts. At her age Ellen would have tried to hide that abundance. Ellen didn't want to make her daughter self-conscious when she seemed so comfortable in her body. Which had to be good, didn't it? Why should a girl cover up what God or Nature had given her? But, throwing the bargain-price Warehouse coverlet with its *'Made in China'* label over the freshly made bed, Ellen worried about what kind of male attention her daughter might attract.

Lily-who-called-herself-Delilah looked so innocent despite her efforts to appear older and sophisticated. And so beautiful —Ellen's insides turned warm and mushy—what boy wouldn't want her? And they were all as randy as young billy goats at that age.

She carried more folded sheets into the boys' room. They were supposed to make their own beds and keep the room tidy. Picking up crumpled pyjama pants from the floor, she sighed, and hoped the exercise books spilled across one bunk weren't needed at school today.

In Lily's room her dressing table was covered in dust. Bottles, jars and sprays jostled for space along with hair ties and coloured clips. Lily and her friends were constantly swapping nail polish and eye makeup, and trying out new beauty products. Ellen had questioned where it all came from.

Lily said some were free samples from various shops or came with the magazines she bought every week. Mostly, she said, she shopped from variety stores and the sale bins on chemists' counters. "You said you want me to be thrifty, Mum."

On the wall above the bed hung a poster of a bronzed young man with a three-day beard growth, legs apart and pelvis thrust forward, his fingers sliding into the waistband of low-slung jeans. Ellen didn't remember his name but according to Lily he was a famous singer and really *hot.*

Ellen smiled, doubtfully. Lily might be growing up much faster than her mother had, heartbreakingly confident that nothing bad could touch her, that she could dress as she liked, do what she wanted, without attracting the evil that Ellen knew lay in wait for her round every corner, down every dark street—even in the inner thoughts of the nice boys Lily knew at school. But underneath she was a girl not much different from the girl Ellen had been.

Ellen too had pinned pictures to her bedroom wall, dreamed that men like those in the posters would find her pretty, desirable. Danced to music that "the olds" believed signalled the advent of a new Sodom and Gomorrah, worn clothes that made her father mutter protests and led her mother to quietly issue instructions about using her knee to temporarily cripple a man. Ellen had passed that on to her own then wide-eyed daughter a couple of years ago.

Toby would have to talk to the boys sometime. They too would be growing up soon.

Panic stopped her breath for a moment. Only a short time ago they'd all been so *little*.

Ellen sometimes looked forward to when they'd leave home and she could maybe get a proper job or try university. But that was for later...years later.

One of Lily's dressing table drawers was open, a piece of fabric dripping from the edge. Ellen poked it back, but it sprang up again and jammed the drawer as she tried to close it.

She pulled out the pink-satin pyjama shorts that were causing the problem, and rearranged a purple lace underwire bra and several thongs.

Lily said thongs were comfortable and didn't show a panty line under her clothes. When Ellen pointed out the underwear visible above her low-slung stretch jeans Lily giggled, squinting back at herself in the long hall mirror, and admitted, "I s'pose it's a bit skanky." Ellen was relieved that she'd tucked the cherry-red sliver of cloth out of sight.

Something in the jumble caught her eye. A small, flat, shiny silver square.

Without touching it, she read the brand name on the packet.

Another free sample? Who knew what was handed out to kids these days, even in schools? And there were vending machines in public toilets.

Her chest went tight and her temples pounded hotly.

Of course she'd talked to Lily about sex, about being sensible, not rushing into anything, taking precautions if and when...

But not yet! She was way under age. Much too young.

Closing her eyes, Ellen shoved the drawer shut. When Lily came home from school she'd have to ask why her *fourteen-year-old* daughter had a condom in her drawer—and were there more? She resisted finding out right now.

Maybe Lily was just curious, or was keeping it just in case.

In case she *did* have sex?

Some parents seemed perfectly okay with their pubescent children being sexually active. Supposed experts said you couldn't stop them; you could only teach them to protect themselves.

But not Lily! Not my baby girl.

Why not? Everyone's daughter but yours? Get real.

It's not the end of the world, she told herself, wandering out to the kitchen again and staring through the window without seeing anything but the blur of brilliant red-purple that was the bougainvillea.

It was the end of something, though. Of Lily's childhood, maybe.

She had to grow up sometime.

I know.

She could see Lily as the tiny, sleepy baby she'd once been, herself and Toby bending over the cot, breathless with excitement and adoration and awe, and terrified of being responsible for something so beautiful and so fragile and so helpless. Responsible for bringing her into the world, for keeping her safe and happy, for making sure she grew into a decent human being.

And despite their many mistakes she'd been a good kid—still was, between the teenage sulks and demands for independence and occasional tantrums. Sometimes carelessly cruel, Lily could also be loving and funny and kind, and was fiercely loyal to her friends. Teachers said she was mature and responsible.

Ellen would have liked more of that shown at home. But Lily hadn't run wild or got into drugs. She still said where she was going—Ellen prayed she was at least mostly truthful about that—and she came home more or less on time, albeit not without protest.

A bit of eye-rolling and door-slamming, and a notice on her bedroom door—PRIVATE KEEP OUT. <u>NO</u> BOYS ALLOWED—aimed at her younger brothers weren't hanging offences. But...

The rain had stopped. After Ellen grabbed a coffee and a stale scone she needed something to do. She opened up the garage and hauled out the garden shears.

When the boys came home she gave them instructions for afternoon tea and continued snipping long, wayward branches from the bougainvillea.

Lily arrived and walked over to watch.

Ellen sat back on her heels, looking up at her daughter in her black shoes, white ankle socks and short plaid uniform. Her hair was tied in a ponytail and little wisps fell over her smooth forehead. Her mouth puckered as it had when as a baby she'd watched her mother approach with a bottle.

Lily said, "What are you doing, Mum? Aren't you hot? Shall I get you something to drink?"

Ellen wanted to weep. Suddenly love was too much to bear. She'd made this girl-woman, she and Toby together. How could she ever let her go? It was too soon to even think about that. What a terrible thing is innocence, inviting the world to smash it.

"Mum?"

"I'm all right." Ellen wiped sweat away with a gloved hand. Even wearing the canvas gloves, she'd had to be careful with the bougainvillea. "But a cold drink would be nice, Lilly Pilly."

Lily looked at her with disgust and rolled her eyes.

"All right...Delilah."

Lily smiled. "Not so hard, is it?"

Ellen wanted to take her daughter in her arms, hug her tight and never let go. Feel the warmth and sweetness of her so-nearly adult body, breathe in the scent of her skin, as she used to do with all her children when they were little. She knew if she did Delilah-Lily would wriggle away, say, "Aw, Mum!" and give her an irritated, pitying look.

Ellen shook her head instead, giving back the smile.

Lily hitched her backpack higher on her shoulders. "What are you doing anyway?" she asked again, surveying the pile of wilted purple. There was more on the ground now than on the fence.

"Getting rid of it," Ellen told her. "It's dangerous."

She lifted the shears and grimly chopped at a thick branch, which swayed but didn't fall. She tried again. It fell the wrong way, and Ellen put out a hand to grab it before it hit Lily's bare leg. She missed but managed to deflect the branch, one of its thorns grazing her own arm and scoring a thin red scratch from wrist to elbow.

Lily had quickly stepped back. "Ooh, Mum!" She winced in sympathy. "That was dumb! *What* were you *thinking*?"

Ellen watched a slow trickle of blood seep from the shallow wound. Later it might throb as the other one had, keep her awake all night.

One day Delilah—who might be Lily again by then—would understand.

STRAY

When the last wave of the day came curling its lip along the broad slope of the beach, a dog hurtled from the sandhills and scampered joyously down to the water. Jets of sand flew under its feet, and it lifted its head and barked before plunging into the white, eddying lace and out again, shaking itself with energetic ecstasy.

Harold moved back up the sand out of its way. He looked towards the dunes, the pale grass shivering stiffly in the wind. Didn't the dog have an owner?

Apparently not. It was trotting alongside the water now, brisk and purposeful, its nose pointed at the sea. Harold watched, his hands in the pockets of his sagging trousers, the breeze lifting his sparse grey hair.

It wasn't a beautiful dog. Its coat was black, but it had fringes of white on its legs, white paws and a rakish white spot above one eye. Its feet were too big, its nose was too long, and its tail hadn't decided which parent to take after.

25

The sun had set but in no blaze of glory, just a glimmer on the horizon, sulking behind a sheet of cloud. Now a patina of grey flattened the water.

The dog stopped suddenly and turned itself round to look at Harold, its absurd tail weaving gently from side to side, displaying a tendency to curl at the end.

"Part pig," Harold muttered, and turned to go. Dusk was advancing over the dunes, a creeping shadow of cold.

His feet shifted the sand as he climbed, his boots slipping with every step, and when he reached the top he was panting. He stopped to look back at the beach and, as though he had called it, the dog came racing towards him, ploughing clumsily up the slope.

"Oh, no you don't!" Harold made to walk away, but his foot caught in the dark net of weeds crisscrossing the top of the dune, and he went down, swearing.

Before he could get up the dog was there, tongue hanging out and tail going like half a windmill. The dog came right up to him as though it meant to lick his face. He pushed it off and got up, mumbling curses.

"Shoo! Go away! Home!" He waved his arms, but the dog just sat and cocked its head at him expectantly.

"Go away," he repeated, without hope. And resumed his interrupted homeward trek.

Of course, the dog trotted after him.

At the overgrown, gravelly space behind the dunes there were no cars parked. The narrow, humped and hollowed road was empty. When Harold huffed up the steep path worn through the harsh, billowing buffalo grass, he could hear the dog behind him, panting in happy imitation.

There was a gate in the sagging fence around the house, but the grass had grown high about it and the hinges had rusted. The dog seemed to think Harold's half-hearted kick as he entered the gateway was the beginning of a game. It gave a delighted yip, and stood off just out of reach, its mouth drooling, its tongue hanging out.

"Giddaway!" Harold said disgustedly, and went into the house, slamming the door.

The dog gave another, disappointed little yip, and scuffled a bit before falling silent.

After he had scooped baked beans from a tin onto a plate and eaten them with a couple of pieces of stale bread, Harold peered through the dusty, uncurtained window and saw the shadowy outline outside the door, its body scooped into a half-circle, and its black, wet nose resting on big, clumsy white paws.

"You won't get anything from me," he told it, backing away from the window. The night was getting cold, and he pulled on a stained and unravelling jersey over his faded red T-shirt before making his visit to the old long-drop out the back.

After he had doused the kerosene lamp and rolled himself into his blanket on the lumpy kapok mattress that gave off a comforting musty smell, he heard a rhythmic, muffled thumping that stopped and then started again. "Bloody dog's got fleas," he realised, before he went to sleep.

In the night it rained. Harold would have slept through that —the harsh drumroll on the tin roof, the gurgle along the guttering and the pattering flow to the ground through the holes. It was the whining that woke him, and the thumping and scratching at the door.

"Go away," he grumbled, turning and humping the blanket higher round his shoulders. Then: "Go away!" he shouted as he sat up, glaring at the closed door. "Get the hell out of here, you dumb bloody mongrel!"

Eventually he got up and kicked the door himself, but he should have put his boots on first. He yelled and swore through the wood, but it made no difference except that the dog seemed more than ever frantic to get in. And Harold, in his thin shirt and threadbare pyjama bottoms, was getting cold. He left the door and fumbled across the room to light the lamp on the table again and pick up the poker from beside the unlit wood stove.

He flung open the door with the poker at the ready to repulse the invader, and found the dog grovelling like a wet rug, inching forward to lay its cold nose on his feet.

"Giddoff!" Harold withdrew his foot and waved the poker.

The dog shivered and gave a little whine.

"Out!" said Harold. "*Out.*" He shoved it with his bare foot and the sodden animal somehow insinuated itself around his leg and flopped down again. Now it was halfway in, regarding him with hopeful eyes. The rain was coming in, too, and a cold wind.

"Oh, Christ!" Harold bent and fumbled for a collar. There wasn't one. The dog slipped under his hands and then it was in the room, dripping on the big, faded mat and facing Harold who now stood with his back to the door.

Remembering the poker, Harold raised it. "If you don't get out now…"

The dog snarled, its shoulders braced.

Harold's hand dropped. The brief baring of teeth disappeared, replaced by a lunatic, tongue-lolling grin.

"Outside," Harold suggested warily, flourishing the poker more in a spirit of invitation now. "I mean it, out!"

The dog shook itself, its paws still four-square on the mat.

Harold swore, raising his hands to counter the shower of water, still holding the poker.

The dog barked several times until Harold lowered his arms. Then it gave itself another, smaller shake, and stood watching him.

Harold shut the door. "All right. Just for tonight. And for God's sake shut up, will you, and let me get some sleep!"

The dog sat down in front of the unlit stove while Harold killed the lamp and climbed back into bed, catching the gleam of an eye against the dark.

In the morning the rain had stopped. The dog got up and followed Harold outside, lifting its leg against the door jamb. "And you can cut that out!" Harold growled, aiming a kick at it. This time he had put on his boots.

The dog yelped offendedly and skittered out of the way.

Harold grinned. "Teach you, you dumb brute."

When he came back, still hitching his trousers, it was waiting for him, expecting to be let in again. He strode past and slammed the door. The dog barked and barked all the time he was fixing his breakfast, and flung itself at the door, whining and scratching. Harold ate his bread and cheese slowly, and boiled up black tea on the primus.

The dog stopped barking. Gone to bother someone else, Harold hoped. Or back home.

He rinsed his indelibly brown-stained cup under the single tap at the sink and stood scratching his stomach thoughtfully where it swelled above his belt. He'd have to go to the damn shop today. And cut some firewood later.

He had a sort-of shave using cold water and yellow soap, got some money from the cache hidden in his one armchair, and stuffed the notes into his back pocket. He put on the jersey again and pulled a stiff, ancient parka over it, because the rain had left a grey, chill day behind it. The road would be tricky, even more unwelcoming after rain turned it to slush than it was in summer, when every car that lurched and juddered along it raised a mile-long cloud of yellow dust.

A long time ago some previous tenant had painted the corrugated iron garage green. There were still bits of faded green mingled with the rust on the leaning walls. The door was long gone, but the roof, in slightly better shape, deflected most of the rain. Harold kept the key of the ancient Buick in the ignition. Even if anyone bothered to come this far, they'd scarcely be tempted.

He turned the key patiently several times and pumped at the accelerator until a reluctant whine was followed by a couple of coughs, and then a satisfying rumble. He backed the car out in a practised sweep and cruised away along the almost invisible once-a-driveway to the road.

"Haven't seen you for a while, Harry."

Harold eyed the shopkeeper's smile with suspicion. He'd always hated being called Harry, and friendliness grated on him.

"What can I do for you?"

"Getting my groceries," Harold muttered. Bloody stupid question. Bloody shopkeepers didn't do anything for you these days, just stood about while you helped yourself. He was glad when a middle-aged couple came in and diverted the man's attention. He knew the owner liked to watch him. Probably thought he was a shoplifter, just because he didn't wear a suit and have a bath every damn day.

The shopkeeper was talking to the other man now, while the woman had picked up one of the wire baskets at the door and was going down the shelves, efficiently picking a tin here and a packet there. She gave Harold a polite half-smile. He suddenly felt silly carrying his own basket, like some prissy Red Riding Hood. He looked away from the woman and heaved a plastic-wrapped loaf of toast-cut bread into the basket. No decent bread these days. All pre-cut and pre-wrapped. Nothing a man could get his teeth around. He still had his own teeth—most of them, anyway.

"Staying here, are you?" he heard the shopkeeper ask the other man.

"Just the weekend. Nice quiet little place you've got here."

"Yeah. Busy in summer, of course."

There were several dozen houses, and a Post Office until the Government closed it down, even a motel. And the pub. The local farmers drank their beer and the odd whisky leaning along the bar, and the holidaymakers sat with their gin-and-tonics and white wines and the cocktail-of-the-days around wrought-iron tables in the so-called garden, admiring the sea.

Harold and the woman reached the counter together. The shopkeeper turned to the woman, but she stood back, smiling. "The gentleman was first."

Harold swung his basket onto the counter. Gentleman! He could see the woman's husband exchanging a furtive grin with the shopkeeper. Gentleman. Bloody cow! What did she want? Thank you, ma'am? She wouldn't get it, he decided, glowering at her.

The shopkeeper added up the bill, placing the items in a box, and Harold pulled the money from his pocket, wet a thumb and counted out the notes. He looked at the change in his hand and grunted. Coins, all of it. One and two dollar coins they had now. He shoved them in his pocket. "Dog at my place," he said. "Stray."

"Yeah?" the shopkeeper said. "D'you want to put up a notice?" There was a board just inside the door of the shop, pieces of paper pinned to it: Wanted—rotary hoe, cheap. Kittens—free to good home, cute. For rent—nice clean house on beach, furnished, sleep six.

Harold shook his head. "You tell them: I see it again, I'll shoot it."

"Tell who?"

Harold hunched a shoulder, waved his hand. "Anyone. Owners. Got no collar."

"I'll spread the word," the shopkeeper promised. "If I hear anyone's lost a dog, I'll send them out to you."

Harold glared at him helplessly. Didn't want anyone around his place. "Probably gone now." He picked up the box of groceries.

He heard the woman laugh softly as he left the shop. The back of his neck prickled. He heaved the boxed groceries into the car and went over to the pub for his two bottles of whisky. He'd drink one tonight, the other the following night, and then be without until he needed to buy food again. These days he rationed himself.

He was unpacking the groceries onto his scarred table when the dog appeared in the doorway, paused for a second, then walked in, its oddly curved tail moving gleefully.

"Giddout!" Harold threatened it with the plastic-wrapped kilo of cheese in his hand.

The dog leapt up and knocked it to the floor, sinking its jaws into the block.

"Hey!" Harold bent and pulled at the cheese. He went down on one knee as the dog's head came up, its jaws still locked on the cheese in Harold's hands. They stared at each other, face to face, and Harold jerked the block away, leaving the dog with a mouthful of cheese and plastic.

As Harold stood up the dog's jaws worked and a saliva-dampened chunk of cheese with a flap of plastic adhering to it fell to the floor. The dog's head went down, its paw holding the plastic, and the cheese disappeared in a gulp. The dog backed, looked up at Harold and moved its tail cautiously, four times.

"What are ya?" Harold snarled. "A bloody mouse?" He hurled the cheese onto the table, looked at the teethmarks and the wet hole in the middle of it. The dog came over to the table, reared and rested its paws on the edge. Harold pushed it away, swearing.

The dog sat on its haunches while Harold unpacked the rest of the box, arranged the food precisely on a shelf, and threw the box into a corner.

He jiggled open the drawer under the bench, removed a big knife and cut out the middle piece from the cheese with the chunk bitten out of it. He looked at the dog, still sitting there, its eyes fixed on him. "Oh, all right," Harold grumbled. "You might as well have it." He peeled off the remains of the plastic and threw the cheese down on the floor. The dog pounced on it as though it were alive and getting away.

When he went to cut some scrub for firewood, along the border of the farm nearby, the dog followed. The scrub— mostly kahikatea, tea-tree plus harsh brown—stopped abruptly at a sheep-fence, and on the other side of the wires cropped grass sloped to bare hills with dark green bush huddled in the gullies. The sheep were distant dots of white today, spread over the hills.

The dog sat by, looking interested while Harold hacked down a couple of tea-trees, sawed them up and shoved the pieces into a sack. Once the mutt went flying off after a rabbit, head down, but came back in a few minutes and started circling happily round Harold and getting in the way. Harold cursed and kicked out a couple of times, yet on their return didn't bother trying to keep the dog out of the house. He tossed it the remains of his stale bread and opened the new loaf for himself at lunchtime. Afterwards they went down to the beach and Harold collected a sackful of driftwood. The dog picked up a whitened stick and dropped it at Harold's feet, skipping off a little way in invitation.

"No games," Harold told it, ignoring the stick.

The dog picked it up again and scampered along the sand with the stick in its jaws, tossed it a few times, nudged at it and then came tearing back, holding it.

"No." Harold shoved another piece of driftwood into the sack. After a while the dog dropped the stick and went into the water. Harold was well away from it when it came out and shook itself. He stood at the foot of the dunes and waited for it to come up to him before heading home.

Harold had lit the stove and cooked dinner, tossing the dog a sausage. The dog was lucky. Occasionally Harold got a bit of home-killed mutton from the neighbouring farmer in return for shooting a few rabbits; on his grocery days he'd buy sausages or a couple of chops and some bacon—and that didn't keep like it used to. But mostly he did without meat. Didn't even fish much anymore.

The dog lay down by the stove, and Harold wrapped his blanket about himself and took the whisky bottle he had started on to bed with him.

A sudden weight descended on the bed some time in the middle of the night, but he didn't even react. When he tried to turn over, the weight shifted and settled on him, and he woke up to find the dog lying on top of him.

"Giddoff!" He heaved at it, and when it didn't move closed his fist and hit at it.

The dog snarled.

Harold stiffened. "Look, you son-of-a-bitch—" He tried to sit up, to push at the dog again.

It reared up a little, its front paws on his chest, and snarled again. Moonlight streamed in through the curtainless windows, and Harold clearly saw the dog's teeth, made for biting and tearing flesh. "Off!" he said, trying to sound authoritative. He moved his legs, and the dog's rear half slid down between Harold and the wall by the bed. The mutt wuffed in his face, then settled with its forelegs on his chest.

Harold grasped its shoulders, tried to wrestle it off the bed. It stood up with its paws on his chest and barked at him, over and over, with the occasional snarl in between to reinforce the message. Then it settled itself down again and made a little snuffling noise, its nose under Harold's chin.

"What the hell..." Harold muttered, and went back to sleep.

Towards dawn he woke again, this time to a thumping, rustling sound. The dog had dragged the bread down off the shelf and was trying to get through the plastic.

"I'll kill you!" Harold threatened after rescuing the bread. But the gun under the bed wasn't loaded and his head ached, so instead he opened the door and the dog shot outside, needing no help from the barefooted kick Harold gave its rump as it passed him.

Harold banged the door behind it—"Good riddance"—and went back to bed.

He didn't see the dog again until late the following afternoon. He was climbing the path to the house with a couple of snapper dangling from his hand when the animal suddenly appeared at the top of it, looking down at him with a pleased air.

Harold grunted. "Thought you'd gone." But it followed him all the way home.

Offered the remains of the fish, the dog sniffed and disdained it. "Too well fed," Harold said. "I've spoiled you." Leaving it settled by the fire, he went out to throw the scraps over the fence instead for the gulls and rats to dispose of.

He finished the second bottle of whisky and didn't even feel the dog get onto his bed and settle beside him. Didn't know what woke him, except a sudden feeling of removed weight, loss of warmth. And once he woke, he had an urgent need to empty his bladder.

The back door was open. Couldn't have shut it properly on his last visit to the outhouse.

Coming back, he hesitated in the doorway, turned about, called, "Dog?" Tentatively whistled.

Damn animal. What time was it anyway? The moon rode high, clouds obscuring some of the stars. He could hear the sea hushing and booming. And another sound in the other direction.

Bleating. Sheep bleating. In the middle of the night. And was that other short, sharp sound a distant bark?

Swearing, he pulled on his trousers, his jersey, his parka, and blundered out into the night. Had to go back because he'd forgotten his boots. And something else. He fumbled under the bed, brought out the rifle, stuffed cartridges into his pocket.

Somewhere along the way through the scratching, clutching scrub, he realised he was still drunk.

He fumbled along the fence to a corner post where he could climb over. A cloud covered the moon, and he could scarcely see his feet. But he could hear the dog clearly now, the joyous yipping above the panic-stricken bleating of sheep. He ran across the paddock, breathing harshly, his chest tight, stumbling in the dark.

Then the cloud shifted and the moonlight washed over the paddock and he saw a shifting huddle of white bailed up in a corner against the fence, and several white shapes lying on the ground outside the frightened mob. Two more were racing madly away along the fence line, and after them a black shadow with white blurring feet, moving like a dream—beautiful, fast, deadly.

"No!" Harold shouted, and ran towards the shadow, waving the empty gun. "No—you stupid bastard! You bloody mongrel!"

He tripped, found a stone near his hand and picked it up, threw it ineffectually. The moonlight gave the dog's coat a silver sheen it had never had in daylight as it flowed after the sheep, a rippling symphony of muscle and power and speed.

Sitting on the ground, Harold pulled the cartridges from his pocket and loaded the gun with shaking fingers, closed the breech with a snap. He stood up. The two sheep separated, heading with their ungainly rocking gait in different directions across the paddock, and as the dog sheered off after one of them Harold put two fingers in his mouth and blew a long, desperate, imperative whistle.

He wouldn't have believed it. *I'm drunk*, he reminded himself as though it couldn't be happening. But it was. The dog stopped almost in mid-stride and looked over to him, tail up, ears alert. Even at a distance the moonlight was so clear Harold could almost see the enquiring look in its cocked head and dark, shining eyes. Then it trotted towards him, its silly tail waving. Harold lifted the rifle and sighted it.

The dog came closer. It stopped about ten yards from him, and Harold took a deep breath, his finger moving on the trigger. But he paused as the dog suddenly darted forward, ducking its head.

It came up with a stick in its mouth. Harold muttered something obscene.

The dog did a playful, skipping scamper towards him, and as Harold focused the gun on its head, it reached him and looked up, its eyes luminous, the stick still held in its blood-soaked jaws.

"All right," Harold said. He put out his hand and took the stick and threw it as far as he could.

The dog gave one ecstatic, shouting bark and raced away after it in the moonlight, described a graceful half-circle and picked it up on the run without breaking stride, then came streaking back to Harold, grinning around the stick, bursting with foolish canine pride, coming to a skidding stop before sinking on its haunches in front of him.

Harold aimed between its eyes and pulled the trigger.

The dog jerked, sat for a moment, then dropped the stick and with a small whimper sank down slowly until its nose rested between Harold's feet. Blood ran from its head and flowed over its nose and onto the cracked leather toes of Harold's boots.

"Stupid dog," Harold said, lowering the gun. Then, shouting, "You bloody *stupid* idiot dog!" He kicked at it viciously, his boot thudding against its shoulder, its chest, its stomach, and the dog's legs twitched as though it were about to get up and shake itself and start that ridiculous tail-wagging again.

"Dumb bastard of a mongrel," Harold said tiredly, and put down the gun. "There you are, see?" He sat on the ground and took the bloodied head in his hands, letting it lie in his lap, bleeding all over his trousers. "Good dog," he said, his hands trembling as they fondled the warm, silky black ears. "Good dog."

THE WRITER IN SEARCH OF A STORY

The story waits in the shadows. The writer has a deadline and the story wants to be told, but the story has patience. It is in no hurry.

The writer gets up from the computer and goes for a walk, hoping the story will emerge and show itself, or at least give some hint of its being—a scent, a slight stirring, a restless rustling or a small anticipatory shiver.

He crosses the road and walks a while before choosing a tree-lined street. He thinks he sees the story in a spreading elm with arthritic knees and elbows, its leaves yellowed by a cold autumn, pirouetting in the wind and coasting down one by one to huddle with others heaped against the shelter of a grey stone wall.

But the writer is mistaken. There is no story here.

These streets are all unfamiliar. The writer is the fortunate temporary tenant of a much desired residency in a strange city, due to the generosity of a trust dedicated to providing writers with a private, quiet and lonely place in which to write.

A woman is coming towards him, led by a small scruffy dog. She smiles at the writer briefly as they pass, and says, "Good afternoon." Neither she nor the dog are memorable and the writer soon forgets them.

The woman was once the centre of a scandal involving a politician, a well-known radio personality and a strip club. Her photograph appeared in the newspapers almost daily for several weeks. Now she lives alone with her dog in an ugly, little flat and never reads the paper, or watches the news on her small-screen TV.

The writer passes an old villa set below the level of the path and of its moss-greened brick wall. The house has been subjected to renovation, its weathered wood coated with glistening white paint, and the original windows replaced with floor-length glass. In one room the writer sees a large, unmade bed—white sheets turned back in a cornerwise heap over a flowered duvet on one side, the other side primly tucked in. A dressing table is littered with oddly shaped bottles and jars, while dispirited purplish roses wilt in a narrow vase, and a necklace of some sort spills from a small overfilled basket.

Why, the writer asks himself, does anyone want their bedroom exposed to the world walking by?

Further on, he hears a young child crying. A muffled female voice is drowned by the sound of the child's wailing. The child has recently become a toddler. Its father works night shifts at a hospital, and the mother has a part-time cleaning job in the mornings, taking the child along. They are Samoan and want their child to have an education, a good wife and a good job. The child does not want an afternoon sleep, but is fractious and likely to wake the father. The woman has decided to take it out in its stroller. She is trying to insert the child into a warm jacket which it is determined not to wear. The mother is nearing breaking point.

Ignoring an uncomfortable sensation in his chest brought on by the howling infant, the writer hurries on, while the story lags behind...

At another house the writer lingers for a few seconds. Hunkered between two neat gardens with tall, though severely clipped hedges sits a tumbledown dwelling with a rusted roof and weatherboard walls almost bare of paint, the remains so faded that any original colour defies identification. The dirty windows are hung with what appear to be sheets, sagging and showing a peculiar shade between grey and brown. There is no intimation of life behind the sheets, nor in the overgrown weeds and a few unidentifiable shrubs, making a last desperate gasp to escape through the gap-toothed fence. The hedges on this side have run amok, and the narrow spaces between them and the house are filled with piles of ancient bricks and rotting timber, as if someone had once aspired to rescue the house from its squalid putrefaction. Futility seeps from its cracked weatherboards and leaky guttering.

A panting jogger passes by, skirting the writer as he contemplates the ruined house. It must once have had a life, inhabitants who laughed and cried and fought and raised children – certainly there must have been children. People had lived here through two world wars and a depression. How many families has it seen come and go, how many triumphs and tragedies, how many petty squabbles and furious arguments, passionate loves or passive ones, splintered relationships, broken men and women and brave battlers? How much drama and gladness and sorrow has the house seen in its lifetime? And who, if anyone, dwells now within its decaying walls?

"God, no!" the writer groans. He is looking for a story, not a damned cliché.

Turning away with a grimace, the writer thinks he sees movement on the corner opposite as the story slips out of sight.

He steps hurriedly onto the road, and immediately leaps back as a large black car snarls into his vision with an irritated blast of its horn and a shriek of brakes.

"Jesus!" The writer trips on the kerb, just saves himself from falling, and claps a hand over his jack-hammering heart.

The driver lifts two fingers and sweeps off along the street, leaving the writer with shaking knees, gulping for breath. He takes a minute to recover. Then, carefully looking both ways, he dares to cross the street and head around the corner, but there is now no sign of the story, only an old Chinese man tottering along on the other side of the road. His wrinkled face records his violent experiences during China's Cultural Revolution, when he was banished to the Gobi Desert.

The writer feels in need of something to steady himself. What might have happened if he'd been less quick to jump out of harm's way, or the driver's reactions had been less immediate? The driver's contemptuous gesture riles him, and the writer is sure the car was travelling too fast. However, to be fair, he must admit to being careless himself.

If the worst had happened, who would mourn him? With a writer's imagination, he imagines himself lying dead and cold and chillingly pale while his family gathers round his coffin—or, as funeral directors like to call it, "the casket". The word brings to the writer's mind some kind of treasure chest, like pirate loot rather than decaying flesh. The writer despises euphemisms.

His mother would be there of course. Perhaps crying. Or stoically not crying. She would have arranged everything, made sure his suit was dry-cleaned before handing it over to the funeral director to dress him. Probably she'd find the awful tie she'd given him last Christmas and have them put it around his cold, dead neck. His older brother would turn up with his wife and two teenage sons, and his sister would fly over from Australia where she was some kind of manager dealing with mortgages in a major bank. The writer can never remember which one. She and the sister-in-law would exchange cool kisses and vie with each other to "look after" his mother, who would be irritated by their solicitude but suffer it in the cause of family harmony.

His brother, certain that his wife and sister were fast friends, would remark heartily with a condemning glance at his sister that it was a pity they met so seldom, mainly at funerals and alternative Christmases. At one such occasion, after a few glasses of indifferent wine, the writer's sister confided in the writer that their brother's wife was "a nitwit who thinks she's somehow entitled to be condescending because she's got a wedding ring and has given birth to a couple of unattractive brats with no manners and no brains."

The writer found this judgement harsh but not necessarily untrue; he tends to avoid his nephews. Half-grown, uncompleted humanity induces in him a combination of boredom and incomprehension. Being a high school teacher, he has endured more than enough of their company.

He believes, without evidence, that his sister is a lesbian, and that this is why she is unmarried and lives in Australia. Their mother might have reluctantly accepted this in the cause of family unity. Their father would have tried to ignore it if the fact were not openly stated, but if that became impossible...

His dead father is still a mystery to the writer, never predictable. He would perhaps have been inclined to cut his daughter off with much sound and fury, even withhold the proverbial penny to fly with. Distracted here, the writer wonders how many pennies or cents or dollars his father had accumulated over a lifetime of servitude in the small cogs of Big Business, and whether the penny to fly with is the same penny withheld from errant offspring. He must remember to look it up when he gets back to his computer.

The story trudging beside him sighs, but the writer doesn't hear.

The writer is not married, and does not have a partner, male or female. He has passed through several relationships with women but none made the grade of permanence.

In any case, he dislikes the word "partner" for its banality and its ambiguity in certain situations. He might in another age have taken a mistress, as was once the privilege of poets and others of a creative bent or some sort of fame. When in his romantic twenties, the notion appealed to him with its flavour of Bohemianism. But already the word had passed its best-before date. He regrets its demise.

Now in his forties, he is well-established as a presence in the literary world. His reputation has been built on the foundation of an early award for a "First Book of Poetry", much admired by readers of literary magazines, and given an enthusiastic review in *The Listener*. It was rumoured that the winner should have been a more experienced, well-known older poet who had suffered a falling-out with one of the eminent literary men on the judging panel, thus annihilating his chances.

This the writer prefers not to believe. Besides impugning the integrity of the judges, the rumour naturally offended his pride, and he set about trying to prove himself worthy of the honour bestowed, not to mention the useful amount of money.

The writer has found that useful amounts of money are rare in the literary world, and that the number of dollars likely to accrue to the average poet is unlikely to amount to many more than the number of teeth in the mouth of the average hen. Short stories do little better. The writer has for some years been trying to teach his high-schoolers rudimentary English and instil in them an appreciation of literature. But his art, he tells intimate friends—and lovers who show signs of expecting more of him than he wishes to give—is his life.

In fact, the writer discovered an urge to create poetry only after he began teaching it.

In *actual* fact, his first poem was an elegy for his father, written by hand on a lined pad. Surprised at himself, he'd toyed for several seconds with the possibility of reading it at the funeral, and later thanked God, if such a being existed, that he'd had the sense to reject the maudlin thought. He was content to help his older brother compose a fitting eulogy and with some regret consigned his first effort at the poetic form, suitably torn apart and screwed into an untidy ball, to the dustbin. Not because it was a bad poem (although he now had no doubt it was, like most first efforts and particularly those that might be categorised as therapy), but because he did not want his grief made public. He and his father had rarely understood each other, and the writer had in his own adolescent arrogance felt entitled to regard his sire with a sort of pitying disdain. Yet, love in the end prevailed.

And the desire to write poetry persisted.

His works continue to appear in literary magazines and he has produced a growing number of short stories, with some success in getting published. Enough, indeed, to interest a respected small publisher in a proposed volume of these literary gems, and a signed contract on the promise of a few new stories to make the volume a respectable size. This, and his expressed desire to work on a novel, were factors in his successful bid to obtain the writers' residency.

The novel, he hopes, will be published locally and overseas, and if successful may bring in some real money. In pursuit of this, he has taken extended leave from his teaching job and hopes never to return to the profession.

Realistically he knows that hope is a chimera, a false genie promising riches and a life of ease, but authors are not noted for ordinary ambitions. The writer's desire for a living wage earned from his talent is at least equalled by his desire for the respect of his peers: other writers, reviewers, academics and those few members of the general public who appreciate the importance of words that can sing and dance, evoke tears and laughter and excitement, explore the mysteries of life and love and death, of God and no-god, humanity and inhumanity; words that comfort or discomfort, that accuse or plead, that tempt and repel, that can encompass a whole life on a single page, distil a universal truth in a few lines.

The writer lives only to make his words immortal. To write perhaps just a single phrase the world will remember. Even if it should forget his name.

But right now the writer is interested only in finding his story and a cup of coffee. After the incident of the car, he remains shaken and wishes to find someplace he can sit down, imbibe some revivifying liquid and recover from his fright. The writer has never pretended to be a tough guy, much to the disappointment of his father, who had hoped he would make the school rugby team and distinguish himself therein as his elder brother had, his team picture hanging alongside others in the school hall as an encouragement to those coming after him.

The writer had not distinguished himself in any way. Not even academically, which his father might have regarded as a consolation prize, but perhaps better than nothing. The writer sometimes suspects his mother of an indiscretion. He is not much like either his father or his brother, both sturdy, handsome men with black curls and dark green-brown eyes. The writer has his mother's blue, washed-denim eyes and thin, indeterminate hair, in the writer's case not so much receding now as giving up the struggle, his forehead growing higher daily. He hopes it gives him a distinguished intellectual appearance, but his remaining hair being increasingly sparse, he has bought several hats appropriate to various milieux. He does not want to follow a prevailing trend in art and literary circles to let surviving strands grow long in some kind of compensation for a bald pate. Today he wears a grey felt fedora with a narrow brim. It does not sport a feather. As the autumn wind is traversing the streets at a pace rather faster than his own, he is obliged now and then to raise a hand to retain the hat and his dignity.

The story still has not shown itself. The writer is now almost at the end of the long street that slopes downhill to a road where cars are crossing every second, and he sees buildings that indicate commerce is going on there.

He quickens his step and reaches a small shopping centre. Here he finds a dozen or so businesses including a bank and a junk shop claiming in curlicued lettering to sell "antiques and collectables". Another sign indicates a vegetarian cafe and he makes for that. The story is following close behind him, but when he feels the prickling between his shoulders and glances back, it has vanished into the junk shop to browse among delicately carved and supremely uncomfortable chairs, splay-footed occasional tables, and glass cases where tarnished pieces of outdated jewellery languish. Here many stories huddle, whispering in dusty corners.

Settling itself on a small, hard Victorian sofa with blackened varnish and faded blue velvet upholstery, the story inhales the delicious smell of age and decay and forgotten pasts while it waits for the writer to order his coffee.

The writer is not a vegetarian and he hopes the cafe serves actual coffee, not caffeine-free stuff pretending to be the real thing.

The young woman behind the counter, wearing a gold-embroidered sari although she is a fair-skinned blonde, gives a gently forgiving smile and assures him their coffee is the best Fair-Trade brand. The writer forbears to roll his eyes, selects a lemon muffin, rejecting a bran one, and settles in a booth while she brews.

The coffee is strong and hot and satisfactory, and for a few minutes the writer forgets about the story until something briefly shadows the narrow doorway, and he looks up with a flash of hope.

A middle-aged Indian couple enters and greets the girl behind the counter by name. She is Felicia, and the writer reflects that, like the sari, it seems anomalous.

Felicia addresses the couple in what appears to be fluent Hindi—or perhaps Gujarati. Or Urdu. The writer is aware that India harbours a forest of languages and cultures, numbering something in the hundreds. The man and woman conduct a vivacious conversation in musical, staccato English, laced with their native tongue, while they choose from the glass case a slice of carrot cake and a blueberry muffin, and Felicia makes them tea in a small, rotund pot. The writer, watching them slide into a booth, doesn't notice the story peeking in the doorway, nor hear its shy, urgent whisper against the rattle and roar of a bus passing by outside.

The couple live nearby, after a lifetime spent in Fiji teaching. Their son brought them to live in New Zealand where he has established a small, successful computer repair business. Fluent English speakers, they miss their home island and their old neighbours and friends. They like to visit the cafe to chat with Felicia and help her practise their language. During her post-graduate OE, Felicia spent several months at the feet of a female guru in an ashram near the Himalayas.

The writer finishes his coffee and leaves the café. The story, growing impatient, flips the fedora from his head, and the wind gleefully spins the hat a couple of times and sends it flying towards the middle of the road among the relentless procession of cars.

For an instant it touches down on the windscreen of a yellow Nissan. The startled driver swerves, the car narrowly missing a bus stop sign and leaping onto the kerb before the driver wrenches it back into line, where the engine stalls, halting the traffic behind. The writer has been holding his breath, expecting to hear from somewhere down the crocodile line of abruptly stopped cars a thump and a crunch.

He is vaguely disappointed when none occurs. Writers find inspiration in drama—discord, destruction, despair and, best of all, death.

His hat lies unhurt but endangered on the white centreline, and he dares to venture onto the road, holding up a commanding hand—Moses crossing the Red Sea. He snatches up the hat and hurries back to the safety of the footpath with a nod to the driver of the yellow car, a white blur behind the glass of the windscreen. In his haste he fails to notice if the driver is male or female.

Realising he is now halfway around an extensive block, the writer decides to not retrace his steps and sets off again. If he stops thinking about finding a story, perhaps his subconscious will eventually provide one. Worrying at it like a dog with a stuffed toy may destroy it rather than encourage it to take visible shape.

The story trails behind him. Once it takes a short detour along a cul-de-sac, attracted by a billboard offering a house for sale. The couple who own the house parted recently and the wife has initiated a divorce. She plans to find a flat in a better suburb and live a different life.

The couple's grown children are devastated at the loss of their childhood home no less than the breakup of their parents' marriage not long after their father took a well-earned bonus and stopped working. He too is devastated, having had no previous inkling that his wife was dissatisfied with their mainly uneventful retirement. The wife is unable or unwilling to explain her decision. Mere boredom does not seem an adequate excuse, and yet on waking every day she feels its deadening weight, that grows progressively throughout each day. She is secretly excited at the prospect of changing her life. Guilt is a small price to pay for the freedom to enjoy being reckless.

The story lingers, for a story is always eager to find out what happens next, but it feels an obligation to the writer and leaves the house to its own untold story.

Bouncing along, with a couple of cartwheels on the way, the story soon catches up with the writer. The writer turns, fancying he hears a breathless sound behind him, but sees only an empty street. Behind a fence a dog barks deeply several times, then growls as the writer resumes his journey past the fence, with a nervous glance to make sure the fence is high and the gate secure enough to keep the animal confined. He has never written a story about a dog and has no intention of doing so, although he once owned a fox terrier.

It was offered to him by a friend whose family was moving to Australia. The writer was then twelve years old and would have liked the dog to sleep in his room but his mother decreed the dog remain outside. His father tolerated it, but while making a kennel for it had grumped that if they were going to have a dog it might as well be a real one, big enough to scare off burglars. When it caught a rat and shook it to death the writer's father laughed and deigned to give the dog a pat and call him, "Not such a useless mutt." The writer remembers feeling slightly sick.

His father gave the terrier's ear a friendly tug, making it yelp, and squeezed his son's shoulder in a congratulatory way, making the sickness fade under a wave of pride.

The neighbours complained when the dog killed all their cat's kittens, and to keep the peace the writer's parents had the dog put down, only telling him after the fact. His father again clasped his shoulder, telling him he understood the boy's grief but that was life. He must not cry any more.

He did not understand, the boy knew. He stopped crying and escaped his father's hand to run, and run, out of the gate, along the streets, running until he reached one he didn't know, and collapsed, swallowing great gobs of breath, onto a strange lawn to sit brooding and hating until hunger and the owner of the lawn drove him home. His mother silently dished up his dinner and his father retired behind a newspaper, ignoring him.

His father would have approved of the barking dog behind the fence.

Shoulders hunched against the wind, the writer detours off the path onto a driveway dividing the grassed berm, to avoid a man wielding a small chainsaw on an over-exuberant tree. The tree's copiously clothed branches have become an obstruction to pedestrians. Kicking away the severed remains, the man looks around and sees the writer. He turns off the motor and begins shoving the greenery, still looking fresh and alive, into a heap. "Sorry about this," he says to the writer. "Going for a walk?"

"Yes." How does the man know he does not have business of some kind, calling on a client? Why assume that he is merely walking aimlessly?

"A good day for it, eh?" The man seems inclined to chat, but the writer is again thinking of his deadline and his story. The story tugs at his trouser leg, and he gives the man what he believes to be a friendly nod and labours on uphill as the clattering brrrr of the saw starts again. The man would have liked to discuss the latest All Blacks disaster. A widower whose children have scattered in various directions, one all the way to Canada, he has no one to watch matches with and needs a short break from his arboreal slaughter.

This street seems steeper to the writer than the downhill route he had taken to the shopping centre, but the sweat on his forehead is not entirely due to exertion. *Where* is his story?

He wishes he had spent more of his precious time in the residency on the bird in his hand, ie the book of short stories under contract with a promised advance upon delivery of the entire manuscript.

But the lure of being the author of a novel is irresistible. The luxury of several hours a day to do nothing but write has beguiled him and he has been on an intellectual high, plunging into the early chapters like a diver into a lucent, virgin pool.

Dazzled by his own brilliance, he admires every word emerging onto his computer screen, while being aware that this is the honeymoon stage, that on re-reading he will find egregious flaws and infelicities, and embark on a ruthless slash-and-burn crusade in pursuit of a perfection never gained. Somewhere further on he will hit a stony wall and know that everything he has written is pretentious crap or banal verbiage and should never see the light of a publisher's desk. However, he has not yet reached that Slough of Despond on the way to the Celestial City of publication, and he resents the necessity to drag himself away from the novel and produce a short story of sufficient merit to meet the terms of his contract.

He is Ulysses, tied by his own signature on a piece of paper to completion of a now unwelcome task, while the siren calls him to the unsafe but enticing shores of a bigger work: what his brother—and his father if he'd been still alive—along with the great unread would call "a real book".

Secretly ashamed of this unadmitted motivation, the writer refuses to give it room and instead devotes his attention to the all-important story that will complete his promised collection and meet the required word count. Only this one more story is needed and he can return to his greater work (which he dares not label great) with a free conscience.

Like the woman he does not know, who was slowly dying of boredom in the house now being touted like a tart to all and sundry on a public street ("attractive, desirable, enchanting!"), the writer longs for freedom.

The story follows him back to the unprepossessing house that had once been home to a famous now-dead writer, saved from demolition by the efforts of a small band of literary admirers and kept as a temporary sanctuary for lesser lights who vie to bask in the afterglow of his genius and gain inspiration from his possibly restless spirit.

The writer unlocks the door and wishes irritably that the trustees had insulated the house. Inside it is cold, and the fire he built this morning and fed before going out—entailing a trip out to an inconveniently placed woodshed—has died to ashes, leaving no lingering heat.

The story slithers in before he shuts the door. The writer imagines that he hears a faint, knowing chuckle. But of course he is alone in the cramped living room, where his computer sits hibernating on the famous writer's famous writing table, giving him a mordant grey stare.

Without taking his jacket off, the writer approaches the table and the ergonomically designed, upholstered typing chair in front of it. The famous dead writer's chair, in which he sat while banging out his stories on a manual typewriter, has been relegated to a corner by the trust board in the interests of saving his successors from chronic backache. It is a kitchen chair with wooden spindles forming the back and a wooden seat topped with a thin, faded cushion in which is imprinted the famous writer's backside. Or so the writer must believe. He does not know if any recent inhabitants have dared to use it in the hope of invoking the original owner's creativity.

The writer removes his hat and carefully places it on the old table, its scratches and scribble marks still visible under layers of polish. The story whispers. The writer hears. He feels the presence of the story. He does not yet see it clearly, but it knows its own mind, and his.

He does not want to write this, but the story is insistent.

The writer shakes his head. *Think of something else!* he entreats the story.

Nothing else is possible, the story replies, *until you have written this one.*

It twines itself about the writer, engulfs him in a powerful embrace, inexorable yet oddly gentle. *It's time,* the story says.

The writer sits down in the new chair and brings back the word programme.

He begins to type: My father and I...

PERFECT LOVE

At a hospital in Perth a man tied himself by his jersey to a rope on his girlfriend's traction equipment and stood there for fifty hours. She had a ring screwed into her skull, and any sudden movement might have paralysed her for life.

That's love, some say.

In a place called Sarajevo a Muslim girl and a Serb boy were killed in the middle of a bridge between the people who hated him and the people who hated her, though those people maybe didn't even know their names. Their families buried them side by side.

In centuries to come people will visit their grave and tell the story. They've become immortal. Like Romeo and Juliet. Who both died too.

That's what it takes, immortal love. You have to die. Maybe that's what the man in Perth wanted. There were police with guns outside the room waiting for him to collapse or give himself up. If they'd rushed in and killed him, would he have pulled on that ring as he died?

Maybe he was nerving himself to do it anyway. So she couldn't leave him, couldn't get up and walk away.

They cut his jumper in the end. Sounds pathetic. Like a little boy, tying himself up by his jersey, and they 'severed' it when they jumped him and then they sent him away for psychiatric assessment.

His girlfriend's all right.

Bet she walks away now. Soon as they unscrew that ring and let her out of bed. She'll be off.

Feel that ring in my head.

Feel Tommy hanging on that rope. Frightened to let go because how can he do without me? Like a little boy—a little boy who's lost his mummy.

I'm his cuddly toy. His security blanket. He's said it often enough. 'Couldn't live without you, baby. Don't leave me. Won't do it again.'

Sure.

Suppose that Serb girl had married that Muslim boy. Think they'd have lived happily ever after?

Nah.

That's not how it is. How it is, is this: you meet this big, together kind of guy, he seems to know what's what and you like each other and there's little shivers down your spine every time you see him, and pretty soon you're rolling round hot and sweaty in bed and except for the smell and the fact you have to wash him off you afterwards, it's pretty much okay. And then you get married in a white dress and a veil and have a couple of kids, in either/or order, and then he's down the pub with his mates and you're stuck with the shitty nappies and you're tired all the time and he's drunk for half of it. He doesn't shave at weekends and you can't be bothered doing your underarms anymore 'cause it's just another hassle and why bother anyway when mostly he's going to be too pissed to notice, but it's still pretty good in bed sometimes and you're on the pill now so there's no worries.

And it's not really fair accusing him of being drunk half the time, only on pay nights mostly, and often on Saturday after the game. He works real hard and a guy's got a right to enjoy himself. He supports us pretty well, he's good with his pay and if I go out to work once the kids are at school, maybe we can get a house and a mortgage like everyone else.

So now and then he takes a bit of a swing at me, but mostly I dodge and he's always sorry after. Crying over me: 'Sorry, I'm sorry, didn't mean it. Love you, love.' He's not real mean about it, only he's frustrated. you know. The boss's got this fancy house in Meadowbank Drive, cruises round in a big flash car and what've we got? An old bomb that hardly goes when it gets a bit cold, and he spends hours under the bonnet trying to nurse it along. And three kids and school's going to be expensive and if we have to go to the doctor, well, I've got to dip into the housekeeping money and Tommy hates mince, but it's all we can afford if there's been something unexpected that week.

And one day you look at your big guy, this big, cool guy and everyone likes him and you used to look up to him and you see he's not so big and not so cool, and you're the one that's holding him together after all. Him and the family. Because, really, you're the strong one. And he takes a swing and you look him in the eye and you say to him, 'Do that one more time and I'm out of here. Out of here for good and not coming back.' And you really mean it, and looking back at you he can see it. He blinks and he mutters a bit, but you keep looking him right in the eye and daring him to do it, but then he blunders off to bed and next morning he wants to make love before he gets up and you let him.

So you still love him but it's not like before. Still, you knew when you got married that was probably the end of romance, but that's life, maybe it's even love, and why should yours be any different from your mother's and your mates' but deep inside you kind of wish it was.

And after he's gone to work and the kids are playing outside and you've cleaned up the mushy blobs of Weet-Bix and the milk and the crumbs that stick to the table like stubborn whiskers, you look in the paper that came wrapped around the cabbage you bought yesterday and read about some guy in Perth in Australia who can't bear to lose his girlfriend.

And you think at least you're alive.

The only perfect love stories are where everyone dies.

FORTY TIMES THREE HUNDRED AND SIXTY FIVE

She was making the bed when it occurred to her that for forty years she'd been doing this every morning. Making the bed she shared with her husband. How many times did that make? Forty times...forty times three hundred and sixty-five.

She threw the cover over and smoothed it out. How many minutes, hours, days did that add up to? What could she have done with that time? Written a poem—no, a novel, perhaps—painted a picture, learned to speak Spanish?

The room was tidy. Her husband entered, put his arm about her and kissed her cheek. "Happy anniversary," he said. Later he would give her flowers.

He nuzzled at her neck. She leaned against him, turned into his arms. They fell onto the newly smoothed cover, and she said, "What's forty times three hundred and sixty-five?"

"Huh?" he said.

She laughed. "Never mind."

She'd made her bed. Now she was lying on it.

64

ROOSTER

Sir says, I trusted you and look what you did.

His face has got that kind of sad look on it like them pictures of Jesus in them bible books.

I go to pull up my socks. Sir's always telling me to pull them up. But he says, Leave your socks alone and explain this.

I'm not much good at explaining. Sometimes Sir kind of helps me to say things right so he knows what I mean. Helps other kids in 4M too. He says M stands for Modern, but the other classes reckon it means Mental.

I don't say nothing. He pulls in a big breath, and shuts his mouth tight like he doesn't want to say them words he always tells us not to say.

Then he says he's going back to the library with the other kids but I've got to stay in the classroom because the library lady won't let me in there any more.

It's like when I broke my mum's nice glass bowl what Aunty Annie that died give her. She says, What did you do that for? Like I done it on purpose or something.

Hell, I'm too big to climb on her knee and say, Sorry Mum it was an accident. So I says, I dunno. And she give me a clip and says, I don't understand you boy.

I just smile because I'm too big to cry. And Mum says, Stop that grinning all over your smart bloody face. Just because you're so big you think you can get away with murder. Wait till your father gets home.

But when he come in I think she forgot because she never said nothing.

At primary school we had this trip and we went to this farm with cows and we saw the milking shed. They had machines like Country Calendar and there's chooks wandering round. Mostly dirty white but some of them was sort of gingery. And there was this little rooster that was a bantam. He was sitting up on this fence in the sun like he owned the whole place, and he was sort of shiny dark golden with this red thing the teacher called a comb on his head sticking up like half of a crown like a king's got, and a bunch of curly tail feathers all gold and green and blue and red behind him, just about as big as the rest of him.

I liked him best, that little rooster. He wasn't frightened of nothing. He had the shiniest eyes, black with a gold rim. He looked at me when I come up to him but I didn't get too close. I didn't want to scare him away. He put his head on one side, and slowly this pink bit of skin come up over the eye that I could see and this other bit come down, and he winked at me.

And I laughed and he hopped off the fence and fluffed his tail at me and walked away. He wasn't scared of me. Maybe mad at me because I laughed. But not scared. Not him.

I thought to myself, One day I will get a bantam rooster like that. Maybe when I leave school I can go farming. But I was only a little kid then.

One day when 4M had library period the lady put up this big book in the place for new books. And on the cover there's this rooster with a little black eye and curly shiny tail feathers all green and golden and blue, like my bantam rooster, made of gold and green and blue shiny paper, only the little eye's really only a sort of diamond hole cut in the paper and the comb's golden like the rest of him except for his tail, like he's the king of everything.

I stood there looking at him and Sir took the book down and he says, This is about paper-folding or origami, which is what the Japanese call it. It shows how to make things out of paper.

I know about making paper aeroplanes 'cause we shoot them round the classroom when Sir's not looking.

He shows me pictures of hands folding paper with lines and arrows on it, and A and a B and that, kinda like maths which I'm no good at. And one with the paper all folded up, only now it's a swan. He hands me the book.

I found a picture inside of the rooster, and I was just about scared to breathe even, in case I messed it up. For once I understand the way Sir holds books like he loves them and doesn't want to hurt them.

I says, Sir, can this book show me how to make that rooster? And he says, Well, start with something easy first like a boat.

I looked at the picture again and I says, Jeez, where do you get shiny paper from like that, sir? And he says, Try a bookshop.

Well, I really wanted that book, so I says, Can I take it home?

The lady looked at Sir when she went to stamp the book for me, and he says, He will look after it, won't you? And I says, Yes, I will be very careful. I will kill my little brother if he touches that book.

I mean it.

I went to a bookshop and found some of that shiny paper, but Jeez, it's five dollars a roll and I need three rolls because of three different colours.

I asked Mum for the money and she says, Not on your life, what for anyway? So I showed her the rooster on the book and she says, You're crazy boy. You can't make that and I'm not wasting fifteen dollars on useless fancy paper. Go down the shops and get some mince for tea.

I told Mum the mince was six dollars but it was really only five dollars twenty.

Every day I took the book out of my bed where I'd hid it from my little brother, and I tore some paper out of my maths book and made some swans. The first one took a long time and I couldn't hardly understand the book, but after a while I got real good with the swans, and I got six of them lined up on my window sill. So then I made a bull. That was harder but in the end I got it right and stood that old bull up, all big shoulders with his head down and sticking up horns and pointy little feet like they could never hold him up.

I got two dollars off Peter Wilson for my ballpoint pen with a ship in that I got for my birthday, and seventy cents from

Rehi next door for some smokes my dad left behind the bread bin and forgot, and...

Well, in two weeks I got five dollars. Then Sir says, Library day tomorrow, bring back your books.

And my stomach got sick and I says, But Sir, I still want mine.

He says, That's okay, bring it back for the lady to stamp again.

I took the bull to school and put him on Sir's desk at the end of class when he was packing up, and he looked up and says, Hullo, what's this?

And I says, It's a bull, sir.

And he says, Did you make it?

And I says, Yes, sir. I got it from that book.

And he says, It's very good.

And then I asked him, Do you think I could make that rooster, sir?

Rooster? he says.

The rooster in the book, sir.

He says, Just read the instructions carefully, like when you made this.

I paid for a roll of shiny paper but the lady didn't know I'd shoved another two rolls inside my jacket. They got a bit squashed, but when I got home I opened up the book at the page with the rooster on it.

The first part was all right and I did read it carefully where they says to cut and fold A to B and everythink until I got his head with the beak and comb and everything, except the eyes got to be cut later. So he looked blind and kind of funny. Then it says, Make a reverse fold from D to F and pleat and insert tail piece G inverting folds at H. But it wouldn't come out right.

So I went to bed and I thought, I'm just dumb. I was crazy to think I can make that, and wasting five dollars on that dumb paper. What would I do with a paper rooster anyway?

But in the morning the sun was shining and I looked at the swans on my window sill and started thinking about waking up and seeing a golden rooster like in the book sitting there with the sun on his shiny paper feathers. I bet he would just about dazzle me with his golden feathers. That night I tried again but it wasn't no good, so I took it to school next day and asked Sir to show me what they mean in the book.

He took a bit of paper and folded it and asked me if knew what a reverse fold is.

I says, Going backwards like in reverse gear.

He kind of grins and says, That's right, so this has to be folded backwards.

I says, That's what I did, but it come out all wrong.

He got his paper and folded it and his was wrong too.

He laughed and says, Well, it looks like I'm no better than you. And then he says, Sorry, old man, I've got to go. Maybe you should try something less difficult.

And I says, I already done that bull and six swans.

He says, Keep trying. And he give me a pat on the shoulder and steered me out.

When I got home I started all over again. First it looked pretty good but that reverse fold got me muddled again. And I just about used all my shiny paper. It says it shows you how to do it. They got that picture of that cheeky old rooster with his diamond eye and his curly tail feathers that look real and there's all them drawings of hands and lines and arrows and A and B and G and F. And all I got is a blind chook with no tail and it's all squashed now anyway, it's been folded that many times.

So I kicked it and my foot hit the scissors that I cut the paper with, and I just picked them up and I stabbed that picture in that book with them. I stabbed that rooster in his little diamond eye and I stabbed him in his shiny golden belly and I stabbed his feathery curly tail and called him all those words Sir says not to say. And I pulled the scissors across the page so many times you couldn't see that old rooster no more for cuts. And then I pulled out the page and tore it with my hands and stamped on it.

And the book lay there with all the pages behind all cut up and stabbed and torn.

Then I felt sick, and I thought, What will Sir say, and the library lady? I wanted to cry only I'm too big. I shut the book and he was still there on the cover. I stroked him, and got into bed and put the book under my mattress. It made me feel better thinking he was still there on the cover.

I shouldn't never have tried to make that golden rooster. Only got me in trouble anyway. Next year I can leave school. No more books when I'm outa here.

Yeah!

YELLING IN THE DARK

That wasn't the beginning of it. That night when the world exploded into glass, splinters glinting briefly and hard under the streetlight, and the screaming of sirens.

The beginning must have been...maybe when Pearl gave birth to Jimmy.

He was loud then—angry, I guess, at leaving the dark safety of his mother's womb. Maybe he'd been yelling silently in the dark even before he busted out into the garish light of the theatre where masked, uniformed strangers took him and shoved a tube down his throat.

Didn't like it, didn't like anything about this world he'd been shoved into. None of us have a choice about that. But Jimmy, he could never accept it. Resented everything—I think even resented being alive. As a toddler he'd hold his breath until he went into convulsions. The doctor said try to avoid frustrating him—when he's older you can reason with him.

Huh. The kid was one huge mass of frustration. Reason? Didn't know the meaning of the word.

Tried to reason with him when he was five, ten, fifteen. He'd look at me as if I was someone from an alien planet. *Non comprende.* It was like shouting into a vacuum. And yeah, I did shout on occasion. Okay, pretty often. Trying to get through, establish some kind of connection. Sometimes I thought Pearl must've—you know. But when he was born our marriage was fairly new and I had no cause to think...well, what I started to think later sometimes.

I suppose it's unfair to blame him for what our marriage later became. But there's no doubt about it, once we had Jimmy, things changed. Pearl went off sex for one thing. They reckon that's normal for a while, but the 'while' lasted a hell of a long time. She was exhausted, with a baby that screamed day and night no matter what we did. Colic, Pearl's mother said. He'll grow out of it.

I thought I'd kill him before he did. I did my best to save Pearl, got out of bed and picked him up in the night, but he'd kick and squirm in my arms and yell louder until Pearl came. Even after he was on the bottle.

Later it was teething, and then a cold or a rash, chicken pox, tummy aches—one damn thing after another. Or nothing at all. Not frustrating him meant he knew if he yelled loud enough he'd get his way. Once he was at school I figured maybe the teachers could do something with him.

What they did was send him to a psychologist. Behavioural problems, they said. Maybe Attention Deficit Disorder.

Disorder described our whole life since he arrived. The one time I gave him a real spanking Pearl went spare and then didn't speak to me for a week. You'd think I'd half-killed the boy. Not that I hadn't felt like it. But I'm no child-beater.

By that time we had Sissy too. Christened her Sara but somehow we got in the habit of calling her Sissy. She was about three then and when I'd finished whacking her brother's backside she was wailing, her mouth open and tears rolling down her cheeks. I don't know why she was so upset—Jimmy never made any pretence of even liking her.

We'd quickly found we couldn't trust him around her. He'd pick her up and be all lovey-dovey, but we had to keep telling him she was too little to rough-house with, and a couple of times we discovered red marks on her arm or leg where he'd pinched her. Once even a bite mark. In the end I said he wasn't to touch her at all. I wasn't going to risk him really hurting her.

They always blame the parents, don't they? Sure, we made mistakes, but what were we supposed to do with a kid like that? He started stealing at primary school. When he was fifteen he took a car from the neighbour's driveway and crashed it. The cops brought him home. They'd taken him to hospital first to be patched up—not that he was badly hurt but he was bruised and bandaged, with blood on his T-shirt, and Pearl just fell on him with hugs and kisses and tears before we found out what happened. So what he got for that was being fussed over like a baby.

Of course I gave him what-for but talk about water off a duck's back—I'm surprised the kid didn't quack at me. Instead he just stared, looking bored if anything, as if he'd pulled down a blind behind his eyes. When I asked him what the hell he thought he'd been doing, he just shrugged. I said he could go to jail and he said nah he wouldn't, he was too young. I said that's where he was headed and he said he didn't care. I said it was no picnic inside and how would he like being raped and beaten up. He said he could look after himself, and anyway he wasn't going to jail. Then he contradicted himself. "Anyway," he said again, "it's got to be better than here."

There was no way to get through to him. And Pearl was crying again.

The neighbour agreed to a "meeting" with us rather than taking Jimmy to court, which was bloody humiliating, with Jimmy looking at the floor all the time and grunting yes or no to leading questions, giving a good imitation of embarrassment and maybe even remorse. I was startled when he looked up at the man and apologised, and even more when he got himself an after-school job to meet the payments we'd sorted out as reparation for the wrecked car. Though the neighbour had insurance, and no one expected Jimmy to cover the whole cost.

I made damn sure the payments were going through, and that the kid was really turning up at work. Even drove him there and watched him go into the building. I tried talking, reminding him he was lucky not to be in some youth prison and to make the most of his second chance because next time they might not be so easy to fool. I suspected he'd done a bit of shoplifting since the pilfering at primary school, but he convinced Pearl that the electronic gadgets in his room were borrowed from friends or he'd saved his pocket money for them. I guess she wanted to believe him.

The things would disappear after a while, but other gadgets came in their place. When I demanded to see receipts he said he'd got things second-hand "off friends" or swapped with said friends. I told Pearl I'd like to know where fourteen and fifteen-year-old schoolkids got all that expensive stuff and she said Jimmy's friends had parents who trusted them, and all that fuss about him pinching the odd ballpoint pen or coin or "cool" jacket was ages ago, a stage lots of kids went through, "And just forget it, can't you?"

No, I couldn't. Not after the car business. All I wanted was to make sure he didn't repeat the same "mistake" as Pearl kept calling it. So yeah, I guess I did keep on at him a bit, like she said.

Have to admit, it was a while since he'd yelled at me; mostly nowadays he wasn't speaking at all, just grunting occasionally. I did hear him a couple of times talking to Sissy. As she grew older he sort of tolerated her, but they were never close.

The teachers reckoned he was a bright kid "with problems" and if he applied himself he could have a decent future. But he wanted to leave school the minute he was old enough, and there were more rows. Showed he can still yell—and slam doors and swear a blue streak, even at his mother. Pearl cried, I shouted, and it ended with Jimmy flinging the front door open against the wall so hard it bounced, and by the time I got there he was well down the road. I admit I was in a temper. I yelled after him, "Don't bother coming back!" I'd had enough. Then I slammed the door shut and went back to Pearl and took her in my arms so we could comfort each other.

"You didn't mean that," she said, snuffling against me.

Well, the truth is I did. But I patted her shoulder and said, "Don't worry, he'll be back." The thought was like a stone sinking deeper and deeper into my gut.

Hours later the phone rang. We were in bed but not asleep. We hadn't been making love either. Somehow we'd lost the urge, I guess with age and familiarity. Not that we're that ancient. And I still had the feeling it was Jimmy's fault—all that worry about how he was acting and what he'd do next.

Anyway, it was the cops on the phone, and could we come downtown because...

Pearl was hissing, "What is it? Is it Jimmy? Oh, God! Is he all right?"

Somehow Jimmy had got hold of a gun—from one of those friends of his, I suppose. He'd been firing shots and shouting obscenities in the main street and now he was holed up in one of the buildings.

The Armed Offenders Squad was all around when we got there, with shards of winking glass all over the footpath and the road, lit up by the flashing light of a police car.

Jimmy had shot at the buildings and parked cars. When the police arrived he'd smashed the window of a shop and fled inside, firing back at them. They thought now he was upstairs.

It was a toy shop, of all things. On display stands in the shattered window were glass-eyed teddy bears, dolls with long blond curls, and a couple of picture books. One doll lay with legs sticking stiffly up, hands apparently reaching for something, shining eyes wide open, like a corpse. Jimmy must have knocked it over when he clambered inside.

No lights showed anywhere in the building. A policeman said Jimmy had asked for his parents.

Big surprise. He'd actually asked for us?

What the hell did he expect us to do about this?

A detective in a suit told us Jimmy seemed to have a lot of ammunition; did we know where from?

Hell no, I told him. Never had a gun in the house.

Pearl was very quiet, not crying but white and still. Didn't even seem to be breathing.

Did our son have any mental problems, the detective wanted to know. I shook my head. Agreed he might have been drinking. That was another thing we hadn't been able to stop. God knows where he got the grog but he wasn't the only underage kid staggering round the streets pie-eyed of a Saturday night.

And yes, I said, there had been a family row, but no violence. Look, he's only sixteen.

The guy nodded. I figured they wanted to treat this gently and slowly. I should have been glad, not angry. But I wanted to march in there and haul the kid out by the scruff and hand him over. They could hang him for all I cared. I held on to my temper though and the policeman said maybe I could talk to him. The police negotiator wanted me to try.

They handed me the mike they'd been using. I heard my own voice come through the speakers, loud enough to wake the dead. Then nothing. Tried again. Still nothing.

It was a long time before they reluctantly let me go in, after trying everything else. They were adamant about Pearl though; she was to stay put. When they briefed me they were jumpy but I must have given the impression of a loving, worried father and I assured them Jimmy wouldn't hurt me. He hadn't fired a shot for quite a while and might have run out of ammunition.

A policeman's torch in my hand, I walked slowly across the space to the shop, and nothing happened. Had to duck through the broken window, and glass pieces crunched under my shoes as I manoeuvred between the dolls and teddy bears.

Then I was on the shop floor, calling for Jimmy. My voice sounded funny, I guess because my throat seemed dry, and my heartbeat was like a trip-hammer.

When I didn't find him on the ground floor I called up the stairs, and heard a sort of scuffling noise. "It's Dad, Jimmy," I said, not too loud.

I waited for a few seconds, then began a cautious climb. It was dark and I needed the torch. But once I got to the top there was light from the street coming in a window and I switched it off. I could see cartons stacked all around, and at first nothing else but shadows.

My finger was on the switch of the torch but for some reason I hesitated to use it. I took a step towards the huddled dark form just visible near the window, his face only a pale blur. He seemed to be trying to hide between the corner and a pile of cartons. A long shape on the floor in front of him gleamed slightly in the dim, greenish light; must be the gun.

There was another small, paler shape lying there too. I blinked when I realised it was a teddy bear.

He'd had one once. Slept with it every night. I don't remember what happened to it. Sissy still had several of the things, arranged against the pillow on her bed.

Not raising my voice, I said, "What are you doing in the dark, son?"

A slight movement might have been a lift of his shoulder.

Slowly I moved closer to squat in front of him like I used to do when he was small. The teddy bear lay between us, glass eyes picking up the light. I looked at it, because somehow I didn't think Jimmy could stand me looking at him.

Truth is, I didn't know what to say. After a minute or so Jimmy solved the problem for me. "I like it," he said.

"The dark?"

A grunt, maybe of agreement.

I nodded as if I knew how he felt.

He said, and in the blackness all around he sounded lost: "Why don't they just shoot me?"

He had been lost once, wandered off at a fairground when he was—four? Five? Pearl was frantic and we split up to look for him. When I found him he wasn't crying but he said in just that tone, "Why didn't you find me?"

I had found him, I'd told him then, and if he'd stayed with us I wouldn't have had to look for him, would I? And yes, Daddy was angry.

Now I said, "Do you want them to shoot you?"

He didn't say anything for a while, maybe thinking about it. Pearl, I thought, what did we do that was so wrong? Was it just bringing him into the world? Is this our fault—mine?

"Wouldn't you like them to?" he said. "I'm no good to you."

Something I might have said myself. I cleared my throat, had to. "Look, I might not be much of a father, but you're my son. My boy. Jimmy...I'm sorry." Not even sure why, but I was. Sorry for things coming to this, sorry for the fractious baby he'd been, the frustrated toddler, the furious, unhappy kid, and this miserable, surly, angry teenager who, for some reason I knew I'd never understand, had to shoot up a town to make himself feel better.

I picked up the teddy bear and looked down at it, kneading the thing in my hands. Just something to keep them occupied. "What did happen to Bearie?" I said, remembering that's what he'd called his bear.

"Dunno," he said. "Why?"

"Nothing."

He was quiet for a while, then said, "Am I supposed to say sorry to you?"

"Only if you want to."

He didn't. Well, what did I expect? I waited a few more minutes before I said, "We can't stay here forever. They'll get impatient."

"They won't shoot you."

"If they want to shoot you," I heard myself say, "they'll have to get me first." I've never been any hero, but hell, this was my son.

He laughed. He actually laughed. And after a few seconds so did I. Release of tension or something. I put my hand out onto his shoulder, half-expecting he'd shrug it off. He let it lie there for a minute or so. I felt the bones and the warmth of his skin through his shirt and it was like he was six years old again.

Must have been about that long since I'd touched him without anger getting in the way. When I tightened my fingers a bit he moved and I let go.

He plucked the teddy bear out of my hand and crawled to the window, held it up and waggled it. God knows what the cops thought, but they didn't shoot.

Then he slumped down with his back to the wall, holding the teddy in both hands.

"You can't stay in the dark forever," I said. "Move away from the window, son, and stand up. Your mother's waiting."

He's taller than me now, but when he stood up I took his hand. On the stairs I held it all the way down, until we came out into the glare of the lights. So much light it hurt. Just like it hurt him to be born. And just like then, strangers in uniform received him first. But his mother was there, waiting for him.

And his father was right there too, alongside them. Like I said, he's my son.

GOING HOME

"One of these days," said Rosie, "one of these days I'll lock the door on you, stop you going home." She huddled closer in the bed to show she wasn't complaining really, or only gently.

Reggie stroked her naked hip absently. "I'll climb out the window."

Rosie smiled. "I'll take away your clothes." She felt his chest shake under her cheek, and turned her head to bite his shoulder. "That'll make the old town sit up—the Assistant Bank Manager climbing out of the town bike's window and running home starkers." She bit him again, sucking on his salty skin. "And covered in love-bites."

"Don't call yourself names. You're not like that at all."

"Aren't I?" Rosie reared over him, grinning provocatively. "They said when I was fifteen I could take on the entire high school football cub."

"I bet you could have, too, if you'd wanted to." Reggie smiled fondly up at her. "I remember you when you were fifteen."

"You do?" She collapsed again on his chest, rubbing her hand over it. "I didn't think you'd ever noticed me."

"Every boy in town noticed you, Rosie. Those skirts of yours—how did you get into them?"

She laughed. "A lot of wriggling, take a deep breath, do up the hook and then the zip. They were better than a chastity belt, those skirts. I wasn't ever as adventurous as people thought."

"But you liked them thinking it," Reggie guessed. "I admired you for that, you know. Now me—I've spent my life doing just the opposite. Pretending to be better than I am."

"You couldn't," Rosie said affectionately. She stroked his arm, hooked a leg comfortably across him. "You're a good man. There's nothing you can do about that."

Reggie sighed. "I wish you'd marry me, Rosie." It wasn't the first time he had asked her.

"You'd be crucified."

"Maybe. I wouldn't care."

"You would. Besides, what about your sister?"

"What about her?" He shifted restlessly, easing his leg against hers. Damn Isobel. She always came into this conversation.

"Well, you know."

"I'll throw her out. I will," Reggie said with decision.

"You can't. You know you can't. For one thing, you're too kindhearted."

"Huh!" said Reggie.

"You are. Anyway, you like things the way they are, really. At your time of life you wouldn't want to change."

"That's just it. I'll be retiring soon, you know. Good time to make changes. If only Isobel would make a life of her own instead of running mine. It's worse than having a mother. If I'm not home on time every night she sulks, wants to know where I've been. Do you know, she even folds my pyjamas? I'm not allowed to do anything for myself."

"I wouldn't fold your pyjamas. I wouldn't let you wear any. You wouldn't need them."

"She's such a martyr. She makes me feel like a policeman. Or a judge. If I pass a remark about how the dust from the road gets on the windowsills, or straighten a picture, she goes all defensive and starts telling me how much hard work it is looking after the house, and how ungrateful I am."

"It's her house too, isn't it? You can't throw her out."

Reggie shook his head. "Isobel was supposed to get married..."

"Really?" Rosie raised her head, staring. "Who to?" she asked curiously. "I never saw Isobel with a boy!"

"Not anyone in particular," Reggie explained. "Just get married. Girls are supposed to do that. Once," he added, "I thought she might make a go of it with Cedric Plaister."

Rosie hooted. "Cedric who ran off with your old boss's wife?"

"I'm sure Isobel had a crush on him. But being Isobel, she wouldn't do anything about it. She's like that. We used to play Cowboys and Indians when we were kids, and she'd let me tie her up and just wait to be rescued. Never even try to get away. I had to be the cowboys *and* the Indians *and* the cavalry."

Rosie batted her eyelashes at him. "Oh, you're a cowboy all right. I can see you in a ten-gallon hat with your six-shooter." She fumbled between them, and Reggie yelped with pleasure. Rosie laughed, her hand stroking gently. "Oh, what a six-shooter!"

Reggie's laugh was slightly strangled. "Sometimes," he confided, "when I go to the bank in the morning, I pretend to be the sheriff, going into the town saloon. You know?"

"I know." She straddled him, easing herself down. "This town ain't big enough for both us! Eh?"

"That's right!" Reggie gasped. "That's it!"

"Yeah," Rosie said, "But your six-shooter is big enough for me, Sheriff! Ride 'em, cowboy—yeah, yeah, yee-hah!"

She lay on his chest again. "Your heart's beating like mad," she told him dreamily. "Pittapat, pittapat, pitta, pitta—pat. Hey! It's not regular!"

"There's nothing wrong with my heart."

"Are you sure? What about your Uncle Arthur? He's got a pacemaker, hasn't he? What if it runs in the family?"

"I've had a checkup," Reggie said. "There's nothing wrong with my heart."

"Really?" She pushed herself up on one elbow, staring anxiously.

"Really."

"Okay, then." She rubbed her head against his shoulder. "Sad, isn't it?" she said. "There's your poor old uncle with all that money of his, and what use is it?"

"Mm," Reggie agreed. "But he's contented, pottering with his flowers and taking his two-mile walks."

"If we didn't have to live in this town," she said, "I'd marry you tomorrow."

Reggie's hand, stroking her back, suddenly stopped, "We don't."

"Mmm?" Rosie was nibbling on his ear.

"We don't have to. We can move away, go somewhere else. Aren't you sick to death of this place?"

"Sometimes," Rosie admitted. "But what about Isobel?"

"Isobel," Reggie said callously, "can go hang—"

"Reggie!" Rosie admonished. Thoughtfully, she added, "Would Isobel agree to sell the house?"

"There are old houses for sale all over town and no one to buy them."

"Well...I've only got my benefit, and I don't own this dump of a house. You never did get the manager's job. And you told me inflation had eroded away your insurances."

"Yes," Reggie agreed. "Rosie, I want to dress you in silk and furs and take you to nightclubs and dance with you all night. I want us to leave this place and never come back. We'll go to America—Las Vegas, Hollywood! Anywhere. Anywhere you fancy."

"Oh, well!" Rosie said tolerantly. "If we're dreaming, how about Greece? I've always fancied Greece. All those marble statues of magnificent men."

"Not dreaming, love." He was looking at her sideways. "They should never have passed me over for the manager's job and given it to that incompetent fool."

Rosie sat up. "Reggie?"

"This time next year you and I could be living it up on the Riviera, or the Costa Brava, or maybe South America. Do you fancy South America, Rosie?"

"Not half as much as I fancy you," Rosie told him. "You don't mean it. Do you?"

"Uncle Arthur," Reggie said, "trusted the bank with all his investments. I manage his accounts." He looked round for his pants.

"So?"

"Like you said, he can't use it." Reggie climbed out of the bed and began to dress. Isobel would have his tea waiting. "It would have come to me anyway, but he could live until he's a hundred, with that pacemaker gizmo. By that time, I'll be too old to enjoy it. Someone might as well get something out of it. No one will know until after he pops off. By which time we'll be in Greece. Or South America."

"Reggie!" Rosie said, awed. "No!" She shook her head. "You don't mean it."

"Oh, yes, I do! And it's not as though I owe the bank anything—not after the way they treated me..."

"But what about Isobel?"

"Isobel," said Reggie with some satisfaction, "will be shocked rigid."

He knotted his tie, preparing to go home. It's Monday, he thought—casserole for tea, of course, made from the remains of the weekend roast.

"Reggie? You haven't really—you're not serious! About Uncle Arthur's money. Are you?"

"Absolutely." Reggie fastened his belt. "I told you I've spent my life pretending to be better than I am, didn't I?" He smiled, picking up his jacket and shrugging into it. Looking in the mirror over Rosie's dressing table, he combed his hair carefully across his bald spot with her tortoise-shell comb. Isobel would notice if he arrived home looking in the least rumpled. He straightened his tie and turned to kiss Rosie goodbye.

"Isobel will have the house. Maybe she'll get a boarder. Make his life miserable instead of mine." Someone who'd be grateful for casserole every Monday and fish on Fridays, one steak meal a week and mince and stews for the rest—except, of course, for the Sunday roast. "An elderly widower," he suggested, planning Isobel's future. "She'll probably marry him in the end. They'll live happily ever after. And so," said Reggie the Bank Robber, twirling an imaginary six-gun and tucking it into an imaginary holster, "will we."

THE TADPOLE, THE DRAGONFLY, AND THE SNAKESKIN DRESS

"Did you know," Shaun said, "sharks have hundreds of babies? The mother carries them in her womb for a year, and at the end of that time there are only two left. They've eaten all the rest."

"Mm." Ginette turned over a page of the essay on the table on front of her. Couldn't these students at least try to be coherent?

"Dragonflies eat tadpoles. But frogs eat dragonflies. A perfect illustration of poetic justice."

Ginette looked up, her spectacles slipping down her nose. "What are you reading?"

Sprawled on the couch, with his Nikes on the new silk cushion she'd paid too much for, Shaun held up the magazine so she could see the cover. *Nature's Mysteries.* It sounded like a cheap, cursorily researched TV programme, with a commentary full of implied exclamation marks. *Unborn cannibals of the deep devour their siblings to survive! The revenge of the tadpoles – prey turned predator!*

"Can you take your shoes off?" she said, more sharply than she'd meant to.

Shaun didn't answer, but after several seconds he bent himself over to undo the laces, not taking his eyes from the magazine. He dropped the shoes to the floor.

Ginette swallowed irritation. She loved him for his laid-back attitude, didn't she? Not a control freak like her. They were good for each other the way they were—complementary. Even the age difference. He kept her young. She gave him stability.

She returned to the essay, made a mark on it in red pen. How did these kids get to university in the first place? She sighed.

Three years ago Shaun would have noticed the sigh, come over and massaged her shoulders, kissed her cheek. He might have persuaded her to leave the essays and go to bed with him. She sighed again. Maybe she'd made him old before his time.

When they met he was hardly older than most of her students. She'd felt guilty the first time they slept together. Guilty but exhilarated. Maybe part of that was a sense of revenge against her ex-husband. *See, I can pull someone younger too.* Then she'd felt even more guilty, for thinking of Shaun as a trophy. She'd slept with him because he was funny and sweet and persuasive, and she thought she was in love with him.

Insecurity was her major emotion in those first weeks and months. Was she a trophy for him? Did he boast about her to his friends? *Older women are great-ful. Middle-class mamas love a bit of rough.*

It was so clichéd: she the recently divorced un-wife of the professor she'd met when she was a junior lecturer fresh out of university herself. And Shaun the builder's labourer who'd been working on the renovations to the rundown villa she'd bought with her half of the proceeds from the sale of the marital home. His boss had left Shaun to finish the job when he went off to another one, and she'd made him coffee, set out chocolate biscuits—he ate three—and learned that he'd dropped out of uni to do his OE and that he wrote poetry, something he'd admitted bashfully, looking at her from under almost girlish lashes, and snickering at himself. "Prob'ly no good," he'd said.

Her subject was history, but she'd taken a couple of English lit papers, and offered to look at his work. After he left she'd told herself she was an idiot. His poetry would be mediocre, pretentious undergraduate angst overreaching the author's talent. Or worse, childish doggerel.

It wasn't. Impressed, Ginette asked permission to show it to a colleague in the English Department, who advised sending a few pieces to a literary magazine, which in turn had published two of them.

Shaun insisted on shouting her a dinner in celebration, having been paid the princely sum of twenty dollars for his first publication. They'd polished off two bottles of wine and at the end of the evening he'd kissed her cheek and sent her home in a taxi.

She was relieved he didn't want to go back to university and take Creative Writing. The English lecturer growled confidentially,

"Don't let him. A talent like that shouldn't be forced into a mould. He could eat all of my students for breakfast."

Heresy, but Ginette happily accepted the advice. She took Shaun to poetry readings and lent him books. They spent a few Sunday afternoons reading aloud to each other. He offered to help her finish the redecorating. Payback for her help with his writing.

People started telling her how good she looked. She'd had her hair restyled, bought new clothes—more casual, younger-looking. Started reading women's magazines, buying anti-wrinkle creams that she hid deep in a drawer despite using them every day, and more expensive makeup. She was still in her thirties, after all, a woman's prime. Pushing the thought of Miss Jean Brodie from her mind.

Reacting to the divorce, she told herself. Most women did the same thing. Boosting damaged egos, subconsciously signalling their new availability. She couldn't pretend she was any different. She had always been predictable.

So she'd rather enjoyed the surprise among her friends when Shaun moved in. It made up for the concomitant embarrassment she felt at acknowledging her younger lover. For once in her life she felt daring and interesting.

The local literati took up Shaun as an exciting new voice. She was the one tagging along when he was invited to read publicly with more established poets, and at the launch of an anthology including some of his work.

When he said he wanted to write a novel she'd persuaded him to leave his day job. "We can live on my salary," she'd urged. "No, you're not sponging on me. It's an investment in our future, in the literature of this country."

She was proud to do it, happy that he was stretching his talent. Fulfilling himself. And the sex was good. He seemed to have gained a new energy in every way, excited at spending all day writing, grateful to her for the opportunity. Even the sneer in her ex-husband's smile when they bumped into him and his trophy wife at a university dinner failed to bother her. She was impregnable. That night she and Shaun had made love until almost dawn. Ginette still got hot and wet thinking about it.

She looked up from the page she'd just read but hadn't absorbed at all. Shaun hadn't shaved today, although he knew she didn't go for the stubbled look. She suspected he hadn't washed his hair lately. It looked greasy and uncombed. The silk cushion was now wedged on top of another behind his head. His hair would stain it.

It's only a cushion. You can buy another one. "How are the sharks and tadpoles?" *Let's go to bed.*

He grunted, didn't look up. Ginette took off her glasses and rubbed her eyelids, then abruptly stopped. *Skin around the eyes is delicate,* the magazines warned. She had a special cream in a tiny jar she'd paid the earth for. *Apply gently, with a dabbing motion. Do not rub.*

Replacing the spectacles on her nose, she read the page over again, scribbled a note in the margin: *How is this relevant to your argument?* The student was padding, hadn't done enough research. She gave him a C minus and pushed away the pile of papers with an exclamation of disgust.

"Don't sweat the small stuff," Shaun advised.

Tempted to tell him the job that was keeping him fed and housed wasn't small stuff, Ginette rearranged her expression. She'd begun to develop frown lines between her carefully shaped brows. She stretched her arms upward, lifting her breasts under her T-shirt. "I've had enough for tonight."

Shaun hadn't looked up from his magazine. "Coffee?" he suggested.

Once that would have meant, *I'll make it.*

Ginette got up and went to switch on the machine.

Returning with two steaming mugs, she sat on the floor with her back against the sofa, almost touching his shoulder. "Still having trouble with the book?"

She'd carefully not asked recently. In the early days of his freedom from the pressure of earning a living, Shaun had written several chapters within a couple of weeks. Then it had slowed, and after five months he'd admitted to being blocked.

He'd gone back to writing poetry for a while. Even sold a couple of journal articles and a short story—to help with the finances, he said. "I feel guilty, not bringing in any money."

She'd told him not to be bothered by that, to get on with his book. And he'd yelled at her, "Don't nag me! It'll come when it's ready. You can't force this sort of thing."

Ginette understood he was panicking, afraid he couldn't finish the book. She apologised; so did he. She soothed him— he was right, there was no hurry. No pressure. They made love, passionately and satisfyingly. Eventually he went back to the word processor and worked, but slowly. He was writing a complex work. She'd read and critiqued the early chapters, but now she didn't dare be too critical. What if she sent him into another blocked period? She was afraid of stifling his vision. Maybe when he'd finished the first draft, rewritten and polished it, what seemed now to be a rambling and unfocused collection of scenes and philosophising would be integrated into a marvellous whole.

Lately when she came home Shaun hadn't been at the computer. Sometimes not even in the house. Walking to clear his mind, he said, think through the next chapter—or the previous ones. Sometimes he left her at night and came back to sleep on the sofa in his clothes. "Didn't want to disturb you."

She worried he'd get mugged. That he was drinking too much, which might be the real reason he didn't come to bed. Or...no, she refused to turn into a jealous shrew. Once he admitted he'd spent a couple of hours in the pub. "Research." He grinned at her. "I don't want to be one of those ivory tower writers. Gotta get down and dirty sometimes, meet the real people out there."

Which made Ginette one of the unreal people?

The coffee mug warmed her hands. Winter was coming; they'd have to start lighting the fire soon. She liked its cheerful flame, although electricity heated better. Her stomach contracted. He hadn't answered her. She shouldn't have asked about the book.

"I might use this," he said.

Ginette turned. "What?"

The magazine lay on his stomach. He said irritably, "You think I'm just lazing around, don't you?"

"No—"

"This is research, babe." He knew she hated to be called that. It seemed to emphasise the ten—all right, nearly twelve—years between them.

She couldn't help letting the small, scornful sound escape. "You're writing about sharks and tadpoles now? I thought you were researching real people?"

"This is real life." Shaun tapped the magazine. "Animals and us. We're all the same, deep down."

She drank some more coffee. "Sharks eating their young. Dragonflies eating tadpoles?"

"You don't get it, do you?" The weary patience in his voice exacerbated her annoyance. But she didn't want an argument. And frogs ate dragonflies. "Oh yes," Ginette said. "I think I do." His magazine had a writhing blue-and-green snake on the cover. "Snakes," she said thoughtfully, "shed their skins, don't they? Come out fresh and shiny every year or so."

She had a dress with a snakeskin pattern that Shaun had never liked so she never wore it anymore. She would tomorrow.

"Yeah," Shaun said uncertainly. "So?"

"Never mind, darling." Ginette twisted round and kissed his beautiful, boyish mouth. "You're too young to understand."

WHEN DID YOU LAST SLEEP UNDERWATER?

"Jules' Hotel," said Bee, "is in a lagoon on the Florida coast."

"In?" Gordon rattled his newspaper.

Bee leaned over the computer. A picture filled the screen. A big, round window, and outside it a diver, grotesque in snorkel and fins, peered in at a woman sitting on a flowered couch. The woman wore a sundress, also flowered. She'd drawn her long, tanned legs up on the couch.

"Kind of a reverse aquarium," Bee said. "The fish are on the outside, looking in." Her finger pressed on the white plastic mouse. "You have to dive underneath the lagoon to get in."

Gordon said, "Mm," and turned a page.

"You come up in the moon pool," Bee said, dreaming.

The pool was round and dark, dark blue, shimmering with soft, creamy light across the surface. Bee burst through it and the light turned bright, dazzling. She raised her white arms and swam to the edge. White tiles, slippery. The whole big, echoing room was white tiled. She pulled herself from the moon pool and flopped onto the wet floor. Heavily, awkward.

She looked at where her legs should be and discovered instead a shimmering, bulky tail with two elegant triangular fins at the end.

"Oh," she murmured. "So cliché."

Experimentally she moved some muscles and was gratified to see the tail lift and curl a little. Interesting.

Trying again, she managed to persuade the tail into something like a half circle and seat herself in the classic mermaid position. Her hair dripped uncomfortably onto her bare breasts. She tried to arrange it modestly over them, but it wouldn't quite reach. "I should have a comb."

Irritably she tapped her tail fins on the tiles.

The pool stirred, a maelstrom appeared in the centre and a black head wearing a Perspex mask its mouth distorted by breathing apparatus, burst through.

The diver heaved himself out, plumped down wetly beside her and removed the mouthpiece and mask. "Here," Gordon said. He held out a mother-of-pearl comb.

"Thank you." Bee bent her head forward and began coaxing the comb through the tangle that seemed more like seaweed than hair. With each stroke it seemed to grow longer. She started to hum.

"You're singing!" Gordon said.

"Mermaids sing. Don't you like it?"

"No. I mean, it's okay." He was taking off his flippers, slapping them onto the white floor. His legs were encased in black like the rest of him. "How about some coffee?"

"It's self-catering," she said. "There's a galley—you know, a kitchen."

"I know what a galley is. I'll get it." He strode across the floor and disappeared through a doorway.

Bee untangled her hair with the comb, then twisted it up in a knot and used the comb to secure it.

She eyed the expanse of tiles and tried shifting her tail from side to side, then clumsily turned herself. If she used her hands as well, she could move on the smooth surface quite nicely, although navigating in the right direction took some practice.

She slithered into the galley where Gordon had found two cups and was pouring hot water. Steam and the rich, earthy smell of coffee rose from the cups.

"Want to watch a video?" he asked.

She remembered videos being mentioned among the amenities. "We can see a video anytime. Let's go into our bedroom." From there they could watch the fish.

Gordon looked surprised. "Well, okay."

He held out a cup but she said, "You go ahead." She was a little self-conscious that perhaps her new method of locomotion wasn't always elegant. "They only have two."

"Two what?"

"Bedrooms, in the hotel."

He gave her an odd look before preceding her out of the galley.

There was a double bed and, next to the window—more like a large porthole—a narrow, flowered couch, just like on the internet site. The big round window looked out on murky green darkness. Tendrils of seaweed waved about its edges.

Gordon had folded back the covers, leaving the two cups on a small bedside table. The sheets were green. Bee hauled and flipped herself onto the couch, letting her tail hang down so the fins just brushed the floor.

Gordon reached up to draw green curtains across the glass and she said, "Don't do that!"

"But anyone can look in."

"If you do that, then we can't look out."

"No, but..."

"Don't."

He shrugged irritably. "Are you going to stay there?"

"For a while." She stared out the window. Was that a fish, glimmering in the distance? She leaned forward, a hand on the cool glass, her breath misting it.

Gordon sighed. He went and got the cups and handed her one, sitting beside her. "What is there to see?"

"Shh." She was afraid of frightening the fish away with their voices. "Watch." She sipped her coffee.

Gordon was restless, moving his feet, stretching his legs, then leaning forward with elbows on his knees.

A silent shape swam out of the darkness, loomed to the window, and a round fishy mouth pressed against it. Bee held her breath.

The fish turned. It was big, easily an arm's length. A staring eye regarded them for an instant before the fish swam away, its tail fins swishing contemptuously.

Bee laughed.

"Are you all right?" Gordon asked her.

"Yes. Aren't you?" She looked at him, but soon turned back to the window, not wanting to want to miss anything.

Gordon took her cup when it was empty. "I'm going to bed."

Bee didn't answer, intent on scanning the tantalising view. She could see part of the seabed, with corals and waving tentacles of seaweed, plus a few enormous anemones, pink and pretty. But carnivorous.

A jellyfish, pale mauve and transparent, its centre like a flower, undulated towards her. She could see too Gordon's reflection as he stripped off his wetsuit. She thought he looked better with it on.

The jellyfish hovered outside the window. Bee wondered if it could see her. Jellyfish didn't have eyes, did they? Another one joined it. Gordon was getting into the bed.

The jellyfish slipped away. "How do jellyfish get around?" Bee wondered aloud. "If they have no eyes?"

"How would I know?" Gordon propped himself on a pillow, his hand behind his head, his eyes briefly examining the ceiling. "Are you going to stay there all night?"

A flotilla of tiny silver torpedoes flashed by. "It isn't every day we get a chance like this."

"That's for sure."

"Don't be grumpy," she admonished. "Look!" A long, fat, sleek eel glided by, wiggling its body, then made a u-turn and came back to goggle at them, opened its mouth and menaced with fanged jaws.

"Ugh!" Bee drew back. "Go away!" Forgetting her tail, she tried to stand and shoo the thing off, landing heavily on the floor. "Ow!"

Gordon shot out of bed. "What is it? Are you all right?"

He bent and picked her up, carried her to the bed. Her tail flapped wildly, then settled as he dropped a sheet over it.

"Are you all right?" he asked again.

"Yes, but didn't you see him? Right in my face—it was huge."

"What?"

"Like a snake. A big fat snake. I've never seen one that big."

"Shit!" Gordon strode to the window, cupping his hands about his eyes to peer out. "I told you we should close the curtains." He firmly did so.

The room seemed to shrink. She realised it was stuffy, and very small.

"Are you sure you didn't imagine it?" He looked hard at her. "Nerves..."

"No. It was there, right outside. I told you!"

"Maybe we should report it."

"No." They'd think she was stupid. What were they here for if not to watch the aquatic wildlife? "It wasn't pretty, but we can hardly complain."

"Well, you did insist on leaving the curtains open. Yet that sort of thing...Sure you don't want me to call?"

"I'm over it now. I was just being silly."

"Still..." Gordon said doubtfully, watching her.

"They'd laugh."

He frowned, and switched off the light. She felt him climb into the bed beside her. She wondered if it was a waterbed, and shifted, bounced, to find out. "What does a waterbed feel like?" she asked.

"Never tried one."

"I wonder if they gurgle." She bounced again a little, but there was no gurgle and the mattress seemed firm.

"What are you doing?"

"Nothing." Bee stopped bouncing. She sighed. The mother-of-pearl comb dug into her scalp, and she sat up to pull it out, shaking her head. In the darkness the comb glowed pale, translucent. Her hair was damp but not dripping anymore.

"Bee?" Gordon put a hand on her shoulder, pulled her down beside him. "How are you feeling?"

Outside something brushed against the window, a soft bumping, then swam away. Nothing to worry about, she said to herself. They're all outside. "I'm fine," she said. "Tomorrow we can go swimming together."

"Swimming..." Gordon said. "Sure, if you fancy it." He kissed her cheek. "Bee?" He kissed her mouth. "Bee..." He kissed her breast, pushing aside her damp hair. "Is it all right?"

She moved the long, muscular tail under the sheet, wishing the curtains were open. "It's all right," she said.

"I'll be careful."

She closed her eyes and floated away, through the big, round window, into the sea, among the waving anemones that were like octopuses and the jellyfish that were like flowers.

She swam among tiny silver minnows, and watched a lobster retreat beneath a rock shelf. And then a bigger fish undulated by and she reached out and grabbed it, bit off its head and spat it out, watching it sink, twirling misty curls of blood until it settled in slow-motion on the ocean floor. Then she ate the rest of it, tearing at its flesh until only bones were left.

After a while she swam back to the hotel and looked through the window. She could hear panting and grunting, and under the sheets a humped shape moved rhythmically.

She put a hand on the glass and called, but only bubbles came out, clinging for an instant to the glass before they rose and disappeared.

The shape in the bed moved more violently, and she saw her husband's head, his face half-turned, and another face—pale, female, eyes closed.

"Gordon!" she called. Rage filled her and she hammered a fist against the glass until it shattered, and a wave of water poured into the room, carried her to the bed and left her there, gasping, as it receded.

Gordon lay beside her. He breathed heavily. Then his breathing changed, and she put a hand to his face. His cheek was wet. Of course. They were underwater.

He said, "You didn't feel a thing, did you?" He sounded weary. "You don't care anymore."

"Oh, Gordon!" Bee wriggled her tail and arranged her hair over her breasts again. Surreptitiously she ran her hand over her belly, down to where the light scattering of delicate scales began before they merged into a tightly configured, opaque covering over muscle and bone.

Stroking the cool, smoothly impenetrable surface, she whispered, "I love you."

TEA IN TIBET

Della is weeding her garden, leaving the soil stark and bare between the roses and palms planted by the previous occupant of the flat.

Roses and palms—they don't seem to go together, Della thinks. The palms are too big for the small garden, and Della's daughter foresees them becoming a problem in the future, when they are taller than the house and their huge leaves become shrivelled and then drop. Not just on Della's lawn but also the neighbour's driveway. And onto the roof, no doubt, blocking the spouting.

Della sighs, digging her trowel deeply to root out a recalcitrant thistle. The palms are magnificent, one of the reasons she liked the little flat, but she supposes she should have heeded her daughter's urging to find a nice retirement home and settle into old age.

All right for some, Della had said. But not her cup of tea. She envisaged sitting in a too-small, rounded chair with an inadequately stuffed seat and back, drinking Earl Grey with women wearing pearls round their wrinkled necks and their grey hair rigidly curled.

Della remembers drinking tea in Tibet, made from black tea leaves grown in a place called Pemagul. They were boiled for hours, the liquid then mixed with butter and *dri* milk. Not yak, they told her. Yak is the male of the species.

The tea was salty, like some kind of cheese. Unexpected. But she got to like it before she moved on with her backpack to Nepal, where she met a rugged-faced New Zealander whose ice-blue eyes—even as they met hers—seemed fixed on the faraway peak of Everest. They talked and ate together, two travellers passing the time before unravelling their sleeping bags and climbing into wooden bunks. She wondered later if he'd made it to the top of the world. That would be something, all right. And if he'd died like so many others, his frozen body still trapped in the snow, later climbers traipsing past him, stepping over him: had he thought it worthwhile to have at least tried? Or he might have made it to the peak, experienced that once-in-a-lifetime adventure he'd wanted so much, felt the sheer joy of completing his dream, before the mountain took its dreadful revenge, and he never returned to boast about his conquest.

Maybe it was enough, Della hoped. After achieving a feat that he'd said was all he wanted out of life, what more did he have to dream of?

She had climbed a few lesser mountains herself, both real and figurative. Mostly to admire the view (real mountains), or to prove something to herself—although unlike that still-remembered climber, she'd never been sure exactly what that something was. She was more interested in people than landscapes, fascinated by how different and how alike people were all over the globe, by what was important to them, how they lived their lives. What they believed in, what they wanted out of life. What they put into it. And was there a difference?

Eventually she decided the less they wanted, the happier they were. Not a ground-breaking conclusion. And of course it didn't apply to those who actually starved.

Della herself had never really known what she wanted. She sometimes wondered if she should have tried for a degree in anthropology instead of literature, before embarking on her extended OE. But writing about her travels had helped pay for them, and she'd acquired enough exposure in magazines and newspaper articles to have three books published that did quite well.

In her forties she had become strangely discontented, even slightly bored, when embarking on another plane for another destination, or arranging a bus trip to some hinterland.

Becoming pregnant had surprised her, and even more surprising was the father's insistence that they should get married. Marriage had never occurred to her. Torn between terror and a strange thrill at the idea of making a baby, she said, "Maybe after the birth." Perhaps, she thought now, while casting aside the thistle to attack another weed, the hormones had accounted for her considering the Idea.

A difficult delivery left her feeling wrung out and annoyingly fragile, enough to make her accept Tom's proposal with something like gratitude.

Her husband had a well-paying job in insurance – they had met over a disputed claim she'd lodged after she broke a couple of bones in a minor accident in Kurdistan. So she was able to be a stay-at-home mother. For six months she was happily cocooned in the intricate everyday of family life, fascinated by every milestone her daughter mastered, reading books on child development and childcare, growing sick with worry when the crying seemed it would never stop, and being clutched by unreasoning panic at the slightest sign the baby was unwell.

Then, one day, she blinked awake and became restless again. She joined groups of other mothers and drank coffee with them while the children played and fought and laughed and howled in the all-consuming, heart-wrenching way that children do, and sometimes Della remembered tea in Tibet and longed for the sharp, salty taste and the cool mountain air and the excited babble of a language she didn't understand, and the laughter that was universally understood—longed for the strangeness of being in a place that was not familiar, where she was an exotic guest, a novelty and the centre of attention.

Was being the middle child of five what had led her to explore other countries, other worlds? Della didn't recall feeling overlooked in her own childhood. It had been, she thought, a very normal family, her parents' minor mistakes understandable and balanced by genuine love and tolerance. None of her siblings had wandered the globe for so long, although all of them had holidayed at some time abroad. But they tended to book hotels and cruises rather than, on a whim, take a train from Tashkent to Samarkand or a bus through the deserts of Arabia.

When her daughter reached school age—and how quickly she had grown from a baby into a little girl—Della felt a need for something to do in the hours between nine and three, and found a part-time job with a travel agency. But arranging other people's journeys did nothing to satisfy her own wanderlust.

Her husband agreed to a yearly overseas holiday during the Christmas break, but vetoed any country that showed signs of "trouble" on the grounds that they should not risk their daughter being frightened—or worse. He disapproved of Della's penchant for striking up conversations with "foreigners" and thought her protest that "They're not foreigners, they *live* here!" was fatuous.

"We have a daughter," he explained patiently. "We don't want her lured away by some random stranger she's started chatting to."

"We are with her! Well, at least *one* of us is, all the time. "

"Yes, but when she she's a bit older she won't always be with us. She won't want us taking her to school forever. I don't know how you got away with being so bloody trusting, gallivanting around the world when you were barely twenty."

"It was the best time of my life. And I'm not putting her in danger. She's learning to broaden her horizons and interact with other people."

"People you don't even know."

"How do you get to know anyone if you don't talk to them?" she asked.

"You know what I mean."

Maybe he was right, Della thought, feeling guilty. Maybe she should be adding her voice to the warnings of stranger danger being given in schools. Was she putting her child at risk? There had been times in her own peripatetic days when she'd been in uncomfortable situations, but a combination of assertiveness, common-sense and determination had eased her out of them.

Still, the world was changing, and the thought of her child being too trusting made cold fingers clutch at her heart. The girl was not like Della, who in her own childhood had been fearless and impulsive, forever getting into trouble. This child of hers was her father's daughter—already more cautious than Della had ever been, sizing up new acquaintances before allowing them a polite smile, solemnly watching other children tackle the playground fixtures before trying them herself,

Her daughter grew up to be a model citizen, just missed being dux of her high school, did well at university (history and literature), and became a teacher. Her OE was spent in Britain, with side trips to the continent. When she flipped through the books her mother had written during her adventurous earlier years, she seemed both awed and puzzled. "Did you really go to those places—like Africa and the Middle East—*alone*?"

"Not always alone," Della assured her. "Sometimes in groups or with a friend I'd found along the way. And they weren't in so much turmoil then."

"But…it must have been *dangerous*. At least sometimes."

Her father's daughter. "It was…interesting," Della said.

"I guess."

For a moment Della thought she saw a wistful light in her daughter's eyes before the girl shook her head. "Mad, though."

Della shrugged.

When their daughter left home to go flatting, and her husband had retired, Della suggested to him they could choose somewhere a bit more exotic for a holiday. Perhaps be more adventurous, go off the beaten track.

He looked at her quizzically. "Aren't we a bit old for that?" He noticed her disappointment. "Why don't we go and see a travel agent?"

Not what she'd envisaged.

They settled for an Alaskan cruise. They saw glaciers up close, whales breaching from the ocean, mountains rearing out of the sea. They were bussed inland to see wild bears and moose, and were entranced at Iceland poppies riotously growing on the roadsides.

Della joined in the whale-spotting and the dinnertime talk, listened earnestly to the park ranger explaining the landscape and the wildlife, and experienced a thrill of delicious apprehension as the ship inched between sheer rock walls she could have almost reached out to touch, fighting a mad urge to step out and try to climb to the looming edges at the top.

She tried to enjoy the pampered, carefully organized adventure. *Was* enjoying it, she told herself. But she dreamed at night of noisy dusty markets, of heat, and swarms of humanity in flowing robes, of spicy foods and giant trees and families huddling into tiny homes on stark mountains. She blamed her discontent on the overheated cabins that belied the icy waters and snow-encrusted scenery outside.

One night she took a piece of goat cheese at dinner and when she put it in her mouth tasted a faint echo of something else, and remembered the cool gentleness of Tibet in summer, though she knew the winters were incredibly cold. If she had stayed longer she might have been frozen.

Back home, she mentioned India and Tibet, but her husband groaned. "India! It's filthy and hot."

"Tibet is lovely. Different."

"You have to go through India, don't you? Or China?"

"I've never been to China. We could—"

"Give it a rest, honey. I'm still getting over Alaska."

They never did get to Tibet. He became ill a year after their Alaskan cruise, and never really recovered. Travel was out of the question. Della put aside everything else to nurse him through to his lingering death.

At the end she was exhausted, and allowed herself to be talked into buying what her daughter called "a nice little flat", touchingly adding, "Maybe you could take one of those seniors' tours they advertise. Australia's not far away."

Australia had been Della's first destination when the travel bug bit, but she had soon ventured farther away, greedy for different accents, different landscapes, ancient cities teeming with exotic life.

"*A seniors' tour,*" she muttered resentfully, hauling a flourishing snake of invasive kikuyu grass from the garden. She hadn't got as far through the weeds as she'd hoped, but her back ached.

Still clutching her trowel, she stood up. Her knees creaked. Damn.

But she still had her health. And what was she going to do with it while it lasted? Her husband had made sure she received insurance on his death. She still had some left after buying the new, smaller home.

Tibet was a tourist destination these days, she had heard.

It would have changed. Did she want to join a group of chattering gawkers being led around, the inhabitants expected to show off to them like animals in a zoo? Maybe she would rather remember the place as it had been so many years ago. When strangers from afar were a novelty, and she communicated with the Tibetans mostly in sign language. When they had found her hilarious and strange and invited her to visit their homes, and served her with tea that tasted not at all like the tea she knew. When she was young and strong and looking forward, rather than back.

What if she died over there – on a return visit? Would it matter if she died in some faraway place at the end of the earth? She'd have insurance, could make a new will and be sure her ashes were returned home if her daughter wanted that. Not that she wanted to die overseas.

It wasn't as if anyone needed her. She had no real ties, not even a cat or dog. Although her daughter had urged her to get a "companion".

A long-forgotten tingling began to stir in her midriff, and she felt her cheeks flush. There were places she had never seen. The world was in crisis, but hadn't it always been so, one way or another?

Of course it's mad.

Her daughter would have a fit.

But...

The palms above her sigh and rattle and hiss gently as she walks beneath their long, swaying shadows.

ABOUT THE AUTHOR

Daphne de Jong was born in Dargaville, New Zealand, as Daphne Clair Williams. She has spent her life immersed in words: she wanted to write from the age of eight, and at sixteen had her first story published. After living in parts of the North Island, she settled in Northland with her Dutch-born husband and five children, now adult.

Daphne has published over 80 romance novels under various versions of her name for different publishers. She is noted for the feminist edge she brings to the genre. She is one of two non-American writers invited to contribute an essay to *Dangerous Men and Adventurous Women: Romance writers on the appeal of romance* (University of Pennsylvania Press) which won the Susan Koppelman Award for Excellence in Feminist Studies in 1993. In 2015, Daphne delivered the Janet Frame Memorial Address entitled "Romance and Reality" as the New Zealand Society of Authors' President of Honour.

A major historical novel set in the context of whaling around pre-colonial New Zealand, *Gather the Wind*, was published in 1999.

Her poems and short stories have been published in magazines and broadcast both in New Zealand and overseas, and she has won honours for her stories overseas. Her stories have been included in anthologies by Oxford University Press, New Women's Press, and in a collaborative collection *Venus, Vagabonds and Miscellanea* with other prizewinning authors Ann Macrae and Anna Granger. Her first solo collection of short stories, *Crossing the Bar,* was published in 1998. This is her second solo collection.

Her literary prizes include the Bank of New Zealand Katherine Mansfield Short Story Award (1981) and the Lilian Ida Smith (PEN NZ) Award for short non-fiction (1986).